DEATH

IN HER EYES

CHILDREN OF THE FALLEN
BOOK ONE

FROM USA TODAY BESTSELLING AUTHOR
ERIN BEDFORD

Cover Design by: Gene Mollica Studios

Editing by: Bookish Dreams Editing

Interior Design by: Embrace the Fantasy Publishing, LLC

Illustrations by: TakeCover Designs

Table of Contents

Title Page
Copyright
Also By
Chapter 1
Chapter 2
Chapter 3
Chapter 4
Chapter 5
Chapter 6
Chapter 7
Chapter 8
Chapter 9
Chapter 10
Chapter 11
Chapter 12
Chapter 13
Chapter 14
Chapter 15
Chapter 16
Chapter 17
Chapter 18
Chapter 19
Chapter 20
Chapter 21
Chapter 22
About the Author

Also by Erin Bedford

The Underground Series
Chasing Rabbits
Chasing Cats
Chasing Princes
Chasing Shadows
Chasing Hearts
The Crimes of Alice
Hatter's Heart

The Mary Wiles Chronicles
Marked by Hell
Bound by Hell
Deceived by Hell
Tempted by Hell

Starcrossed Dragons
Riding Lightning
Grinding Frost
Swallowing Fire
Pounding Earth

The Crimson Fold
Until Midnight
Until Dawn
Until Sunset

Curse of the Fairy Tales
Rapunzel Untamed
Rapunzel Unveiled

<u>Her Angels</u>
Heaven's Embrace
Heaven's A Beach
Heaven's Most Wanted

<u>House of Durand</u>
Indebted to the Vampires
Wanted by the Vampires
Protected by the Vampires
Embrace of the Vampires
Loved by the Vampires

<u>Academy of Witches</u>
Witching On A Star
As You Witch
Witch You Were Here
Just Witch It
Summer Witchin'

<u>Children of the Fallen</u>
Death In Her Eyes
Fire In Her Bloods

Granting Her Wish
Vampire CEO
The Beast of the Fae Court

DEATH

IN HER EYES

CHILDREN OF THE FALLEN
BOOK ONE

FROM USA TODAY BESTSELLING AUTHOR
ERIN BEDFORD

CHAPTER 1

OFFICER RHOADES COULDN'T have been much older than me, too young to be standing on my doorstep. His young face had that fresh out of the academy look. The kind of look where everything was still separated into good and evil with no grey areas in between. His baby blue eyes had too much pain in them, giving away that it was his first time delivering bad news.

He really was too young.

I suppose I could have put him out of his misery and tell him 'It's alright. I already know,' but that would have changed his sympathetic heart into a suspicious one. How do you tell someone you already know your mother was dead?

Even as he told me how sorry he was for my loss, the squealing of tires and the crunch of metal could still be heard in the recesses of my mind. I'd known for a while this day would come. But then again, I've known a lot of things I shouldn't.

A gift. That's what my mother had always called it. To be able to witness it all before it ever happened. Maybe if it had told me the lottery pick for that week or helped me pass a chemistry test, then maybe, just maybe, I wouldn't have minded. But knowing the six-year-old boy you babysat every other Thursday would grow up only to die from drug overdose was not what I would call a gift. I wonder if God did returns.

Officer Rhoades was staring at me again. Why was he looking at me like that? Oh. He asked me a question. What did he say?

"Miss Richmond, are you alright?"

I cleared my throat and hoped I looked like the distraught daughter he expected. "Uh, what? Yeah, I'm fine. Just a little bit in shock."

Officer Rhoades quirked an eyebrow at me. I don't think he believed me. "Are you sure? You don't want me to call someone for you?"

"No. I'm fine." Maybe if I said it enough, it would be true.

I tried not to move back when he held his hand out to me. I looked down at it, and my stomach clenched. Touching was a bad idea.

Most of my visions were random occurrences. Sometimes they were triggered by a word or a phrase. Sometimes something as small as a flower on the ground. But every time I touched someone new, whether I wanted to or not, I would see it.

Death.

More often than not, my visions are always about death. Theirs or someone they love, and never just as simple as when, but how. If they are going to die drowning, that's where I'd find myself. Submerged, lungs burning as I struggle to find the surface. And the fear. The gut clenching, throat closing fear that always washed over me.

I wasn't brave. I didn't pretend to be. Was everyone afraid to die? I didn't know. But never have I had a vision where someone was dying with a smile on their face and joy in their heart. Yes, I knew fear very well, and the hand stretched out to me encompassed the very definition of my fear.

I ignored the hand in front of me and looked up, a small smile forcing its way onto my face. "Thank you, Officer Rhoades. I'll be okay. I have people to call."

He hesitated for a moment, but then, with great reluctance, withdrew his hand. The clenching in my stomach relaxed a bit. He cleared his throat and glanced back at his squad car, where his partner sat waiting, before he surveyed me with a relieved sort of look that he quickly forced into a concerned expression.

"Well, if you're sure, but you really should call someone. You shouldn't be alone now."

"I know. I will. Thank you." I backed up and closed the door before he could say anything more.

I leaned against the door and held my breath as I listen to the sound of Officer Rhoades's footsteps on the porch. They paused for a moment, like he wasn't sure if he should leave yet. Eventually, his boots pounded against the three front steps that lead up to our house, and I let out the breath I'd been holding.

Staying there against the door for a moment, I wasn't quite sure what I was supposed to do next. I had years to become accustomed to the idea that my mom would die today, but the pain was still there. The throbbing in my heart still ached, as much as it would if I had just found out.

I didn't know when exactly it would happen. My visions didn't work like that. But I could speculate based on what I saw, the weather, the clothing she wore. Usually, I push my visions to a special place in the back of my mind that I like to keep locked tight, but not hers. Hers, I had gone over a thousand times. Was there anything I could do to stop it? No. Could I have told her not to go out that day? Yes, I could have, and she would give me one of those looks. The kind she always gave me when I tried to change the future.

"You can't save everyone, Elle. Some things are just meant to be," she'd say.

Then I would have crossed my arms and scowled at her. "What is the point of having visions if I can't do anything about it?"

She'd give me this little smile, like I was silly for asking, then say, "I'm sure you'll figure it out." Then she'd laugh as if it was some kind of private joke and go back to whatever it was she was doing, leaving my question unanswered.

Now, I would never know.

I took a deep breath in, then let it out in one rush. Pulling myself up off the wall, I lifted my head, and straightened my back. Enough self-pity, there were things to do.

I walked to the desk in our small living room and tried not to look at the walls. The floral print always made me a little nauseous. I pulled open the dark wood drawer and searched for the folder that Mom always kept in case something like this happened.

Grabbing the folder marked 'In Case of Emergency,' I flipped the manila cover open.

I scanned over the first few pages, ticking them off as I went. Will. Funeral Home. Logins. There, Call List. Looking over the list of friends and relatives that needed to be notified, I stopped when I saw the name at the bottom of the list. The one name I wasn't sure what to do with.

Bart Richmond. Dad.

I sat heavily into the chair near the desk and stared down at his name. Should I call him? Would he even answer? He wasn't the most reliable man in the world. I hadn't seen him since my thirteenth birthday, and that was five years ago. It wasn't unusual for him to be gone. But when he did happen to turn up, he was usually distant, only ever saying a few words to me before he had 'a work emergency.'

Mom told me he was a big shot adviser for a multi-million-dollar corporate head. If she was here, she'd say he loves us and would be here if he could. I don't buy it. What important advice could he give that would cause him to only visit every few years? No, if he wanted to be here, he would. Tucking the loose strands of blonde hair behind my ear, I grabbed the cordless phone from the top of the desk. Let someone else call him.

I glanced back at the top of the list. Aunt Sue. Mom's too-intuitive-for-her-own-good younger sister. She would know what to do next, but she would also be able to tell if I didn't sound surprised. Upset. None of us ever told her about my gift, but somehow, I think she had always suspected.

"Your eyes are so old," she'd say with a bewildered look in her eyes.

If she had to see death and carnage all the time, she'd come out scarred too. I closed my eyes for a moment, taking a shaky breath. If she found out I knew, she'd want to know why I didn't stop it from happening. She wouldn't understand.

I needed to sound devastated. I looked down at my hands and watched the tremors that started to envelope them. I really didn't want to do this.

The door in the back of my mind was hard steel. The cold silver metal was closed shut with a heavy steel lock, a key tight in its opening. I inhaled deeply and twisted the key in the hole where it lived. A resounding click rung throughout my mind, and for a second,

I hesitated. But then, with one sweep of my mind's hand, the doors flew open and I was engulfed.

The images that poured out almost caused me to forget myself. The crunch of bodies smashing against the pavement. Blood spilling out of fresh cuts. Gun shots fired. The sharp deep pain of a knife slipping in. Then there was the screaming. The screaming was unbearable. High pitched wails of unspeakable terror and gurgling breaths. Any sane person would have gone insane by the chaos of images that played havoc in my mind. They barely caused an emotional reaction from me anymore. Sometimes, I wondered if that made me a sociopath.

I dug my nails into the palms of my hands, and the physical pain of them biting into my flesh pulled me back into myself. I shoved all of the images back into the room and slammed the door, the force of it vibrating through my mind. With the visions safely behind the metal door, I could finally breathe again. I took a deep breath and clicked the lock back into its place.

Touching my face, I felt the wetness there and almost glared down at it. I never cry. I learned a long time ago that crying didn't change anything. It didn't bring people back. It certainly didn't stop the visions from happening. But today, today it was necessary. I glanced back at the list and started to punch in my aunt's number.

It almost felt good to cry.

CHAPTER 2

IN MY SHORT eighteen years of life, I have seen more death and destruction than most war veterans. I would rather face an onslaught of bleeding soldiers than face the crowd of mourners before me. Death I could handle, people...not so much.

Mom would have been happy so many had come to mourn her death. She had way more friends than me. Which wasn't exactly hard since I'd only ever had one friend.

Nicole Berman. Or Nikki to her friends, meaning me. Nikki was actually the only one at the funeral home I was happy to see. The rest could go find a shallow grave to lie in.

Unlike my somber personality, Nikki was a breath of Jewish sunshine. From her dark curly mass of hair all the way down to her sensible "got them on sale" shoes. She really was my lifeline in this world. She's helped me more than once from getting completely lost in my own sinking pit of carnage. To top it off, she was completely aware of my little 'gift' and had no problem telling me where to stuff it when I tried to warn her off of any guy who was doomed to die in the foreseeable future. We actually met because of a guy, back in sixth grade when all the other kids avoided me like a bad case of cooties.

I'd been hanging out by the swing sets, watching the other kids playing kickball. I'd never been a joiner to begin with, but it would have been nice to be asked to play sometimes. But by then, I had already been labeled as that scary blonde girl. I had made the mistake of telling this one girl, Jessica, that her new puppy was going to get its head chopped off by her dad's weed whacker that weekend. Ever since then, not too many people talked to me if they could help it.

Nikki wasn't like them. She had been a transfer student, so all the boys were in that new toy phase with her. This one boy in particular, David Bartelli, who was like the Joe Jonas of Ms. Johnson's sixth grade class, was hard core for Nikki. He even brought her flowers one day. It would have been sweet, if I hadn't already known that David would die later that year from a bad outbreak of measles.

I probably should have kept my mouth shut. Probably. Who knows, maybe my vision was wrong that time and David would have grown up to be a charming man who would have married Nikki and brought her flowers every day for the rest of their lives. But at that point in time, David was a conceited little brat and stole Twinkies out of my lunch box every day.

So, when I saw Nikki heading over to where David was hanging out with his other equally stuck up friends, I had to intervene. I mean, it was my civic duty to let Nikki know just how short term of a relationship she was in for. When I told her, she just looked at me like I was the most fascinating thing in the whole world. From that point on, we had been inseparable.

"Great party." Speak of the devil. I loved her sense of humor. It was one thing we actually had in common. She liked to see the glass as half full, but most of the time, she was as demented as me.

I smirked at her when I thought nobody was looking. "Killer."

She giggled, causing the older adults around us to glare back at her. She glared right back at them. "Liven up, would you? It's not like we're at a funeral or something." She turned her head back to me and quirked a brow. "So, how long did you know?"

"Jeez, Nik. Get right down to it, won't you?"

She snorted and waved a hand at me. "Whatever, like you haven't had enough people coddling you already." She gestured to the group of relatives fawning over my mother's coffin. "You could use a break from the sympathy wagon."

She grabbed my hand and led me toward one of the side exits of the funeral home. I tried to dodge people the best I could, but a few brushed me here and there, causing my vision to blur out momentarily. As we burst out the side door and out into the open air, I made a mental note to spend more time with Uncle Bob. Liver failure. Didn't need to be a psychic to figure that one out. Though, I'd be an alcoholic too if I had to live with Aunt Kate's criticism.

I leaned against the brick wall of the funeral home and dipped my hand into my clutch, my pack of cigarettes soon finding their way into my hand. Sweet reprieve. I didn't know if I could have handled one more nugget of the future today without a nicotine fix.

"You really should quit, you know?"

I gave Nikki a pointed look as I lit the end of the stick in my mouth and took a big inhale. She had never approved of my smoking. Cancer and all that.

"When I no longer have near death experiences on a daily basis, I will gladly give up my nicotine. Until that day comes, you can kindly fuck off." I blew smoke in her direction to punctuate my point.

She let out a small cough and waved her hand in front of her. "Hey, just because you want to die young doesn't mean the rest of us do."

I gave her an apologetic shrug, though she knew I was anything but. It was no secret that I didn't want to live longer than I had to. I would have gone off and ended it already if it hadn't been for mom and Nikki. Well, only Nikki now.

"So has your dad showed up?" Nikki tucked her hands in the pockets of her long black dress pants. Her long legs really did astound me. Being five foot two most of my teenage life had me accustomed to always looking up, but at nearly six foot, Nikki dwarfed me.

I took another drag of my cigarette and stared down at the ground. "No." I wanted her to drop it. I didn't really want to see him. Didn't know what I'd have said if I did.

"Well, what did he say when you talked to him?" My eyes snapped up to hers, and I could feel my gaze harden. She wasn't going to drop it.

"I didn't."

Nikki threw her curls over her shoulder and scoffed. "Meaning you didn't try. I keep telling you, sometimes you have to be the first one to reach out if you ever want to have a real relationship with the man who helped create you."

I flicked the cigarette and watched as it bounced across the pavement. She was on that kick again. Nikki was always working on a new self-improvement project, and this year was repairing personal relationships. This was a conversation I definitely didn't want to have right now.

"Can we not talk about this? I have enough to deal with today." I looked down at my right hand and rubbed at the bent in c-shaped scar on the back of my hand near my thumb. I didn't remember getting it, but lately, whenever I start getting irritated, it would start to burn like it had happened recently.

"You can't hide your feelings forever, Elle."

"You know, I think I'm starting to remember how you die. I think it had something to do with bees." I tapped my chin, pretending to be deep in thought.

"Bees! But I'm not even allergic to bees!" The door to the funeral home opened, and the pallbearers lead the people out with my mother's coffin in hand. I moved towards Aunt Sue and away from Nikki's squawking.

She had been hounding me since day one to let her know how she dies, and every time she asked, I gave her a different answer. A hit and run. Suicide. A freak accident involving a blender. And now bees. She was more obsessed with death than I was. Really, why would you want to know when you die?

It's not like I didn't know. I just didn't want to think of her that way. If I let myself think of the way she goes, then that was all she would be. A label permanently imprinted on her face every time I saw her, and there would go my one and only friend.

I let myself be ushered into the black limousine reserved for immediate family and leaned against the door. I knew her. If I told her, she would never let it go. She would be looking over her shoulder all the time, more worried about dying than living. I couldn't do that to her.

Nikki's small hand pounded against the glass of my window. I tried to school the emotions on my face to show nothing as I rolled down the window. Giving her my best poker face, I waited for the usual explosion of questions.

"Come on, Elle! You can't be serious! Bees?" Her face would almost be funny if I hadn't seen it so many times before when I had fed her one of my previous lies. I rolled my eyes at her and started to roll the window back up.

"You'll just have to wait and find out like everyone else."

I bit back a grin when she smacked the glass and let out another muffled "Come on," before she marched towards her own vehicle.

"You really should be nicer to that girl. I don't know how she stands to be around you as it is." Aunt Kate's snide remarks always made my day. It may be mean and unkind, but the fact that I knew exactly how she dies filled my step with a little bit of a pep whenever she got into one of her tirades about my character.

"Oh, Kate, leave Elle alone." Aunt Sue glared at her sister and reached over to pat my hands with a small smile. I quickly moved it out of her reach and stared down at her own paused in midair. She cleared her throat and dropped the hand. She knew not to touch me. "Sorry, I didn't mean to... Well anyways, don't listen to her. She's just a bitter old woman. You're perfect the way you are."

"Thanks, Aunt Sue." I gave her a small smile in return and turned to look back out the window. For all her suspicions, I have always liked Aunt Sue. She was always standing up for me against Aunt Kate, even if her older sister was right in most occasions. At least I wouldn't have to see any of them for a while after this. College was right around the corner.

One good thing about not having that many friends growing up was there was always plenty of time to study. I actually had the highest GPA in my graduating class. If I wasn't a social leper, I would have been valedictorian, but no one wanted to hear inspirational speeches from the death girl. I could just imagine what my speech would entail.

"Thomas Jefferson's class of 2020, though many of you will die before you have time to do anything exceptional in your lives, you made it through high school. Your lives will go on to be completely boring and meaningless, and while your husbands and wives have affairs behind your backs and your children end up in juvie, you will think back to this day when you were at the height of your lives. Congratulations, you poor sad fuckers."

Or something like that.

While I wished I could say I got into Princeton or Harvard with my stellar GPA, unfortunately, the big Ivy League colleges looked at more than just grades. So what if I didn't want to be a cheerleader or a mathlete? Did that mean that I didn't deserve a great school? I could be the next Marie Curie or Rosalind Franklin, but no, they only cared if I had spirit. Which I didn't. Not at all.

Unlike Nikki. She had so much spirit, it was coming out of her wazzoo. But since Nikki didn't have any such high standards, despite what her parents would want for her, I would be joining her at the big UN of O in the fall. Majoring in whatever I found to be the least nonsensical and touchy feely. Probably a lab tech. I could hide in a tiny lab every day and blow shit up.

Nikki was going to be a nurse.

"We're here, kiddo." Uncle Bob, who had been snoring most of the trip, kicked my black ankle boot with one of his dress shoes. I glanced at him and then looked back out the window. We actually were there. When had that happened?

"Come on, kiddo. They ain't gonna start without you." Uncle Bob waited outside the door for me as I smoothed out my short black dress over my knitted tights and stumbled out onto the gravel of the graveyard road.

So, this is what a graveyard looked like. For all the deaths I'd seen, I'd never actually been to a funeral before, let alone a graveyard. I had enough problems with the dead. No need to rock that boat quite yet.

I followed the trail of somberly dressed people as we made our way toward where my mom's new home would be. It was a lot cheerier than I would have expected a graveyard to be. I mean where was the darkened skies, the crows, and all the creepy weeping angels? Maybe that was only a nighttime attraction. Should have signed up for the midnight special.

A hand grasped mine in theirs before I could pull it back. When I followed the hand up to the owner's face, I relaxed. It was just Nikki. No more visions for me today.

Yay.

"How you holding up?" She gave me a small concerned look.

I rolled my eyes at her. "How do you think?"

"Well, judging by the scowl on your face, I'm assuming your Aunt Kate said something rude again, and you're trying to decide if it's worth it to tempt the fates and kill her early." I snorted and tried to cover it up with what looked like a distraught cry of anguish. God, do I love this girl.

Nikki pulled me into a hug in front of the coffin that held my mother's body and pretended to be comforting a crying daughter, when really, I was trying hard to breathe through my laughs. She gave me a particularly hard pat on the back. Her signal for knock it off already, it wasn't that funny. What can I say? I was easily amused.

When I finally had myself under control, I pulled back from her and took my rightful place next to the coffin. The minister was staring at me as if he knew I hadn't really been crying. I narrowed my eyes and jerked my head towards him. I almost started laughing again when the large man startled at my hard gaze and quickly looked down at the book in his hand. My eyes wandered away from the man as his gravelly voice went on to talk about walking through the valley of death.

Man, you're preaching to the choir.

My gaze drifted to the surrounding graves. There were a few family tombs around the outskirts of the graveyard. Each lined up along the metal fence. At least that part of the graveyard was consistent with horror movies. I moved my eyes along the different types of graves and paused.

There in the midst of them, sticking out like the only straight guy at a Jonas Brothers concert, was a tree. Though, it was mid-June, the tree looked like it was stuck in a perpetual winter. Not dead, but not full and vibrant like the rest of the trees outside the graveyard. I stared at the tree for a moment, wondering why they decided to put one tree in the whole lot of land. As I stared, the shadows of the tree grew and widened, stretching out into long black wings on either side. My head jerked up from the ground just in time to see a lone figure step out of the shadows.

A man. At least, he looked like a man. He was blurry at first, but after a few moments, he seemed to solidify. There, dressed in what had to be a pretty expensive black suit along with a pair of dark shades, stood my dad. Bart.

What the hell was he doing here? How did he even do that? Crap, he was looking at me.

I looked away from him and turned my gaze back to the minister. Did they see? I chanced a quick peek at the others around me. None of them seemed to have noticed the man just standing in the middle of the graveyard. A quick look at Nikki showed she hadn't noticed anything either. She glanced down at me as if she expected me to do something.

When it looked like I wasn't getting what she wanted me to do, she nudged me forward with a nod of her head towards the casket. Oh. It was that time already. I tried to keep my eyes off my father, who just watched us from his place by the tree, and reached out to take one of the white roses off the casket. I clutched it in my hand and moved back to my spot, letting the aunts and other relatives have their turn at it.

I hurried a look at the tree and saw him staring at me. He had taken his sunglasses off now, and I could practically feel his eyes boring into my skin. What was he doing? Without a remark to those around me, I pulled away from the pack and marched over to where the lone tree waited.

As I arrived in front of him, I took in his features. To my ever growing chagrin, I looked just like him. The straight blonde hair that swept across his forehead. His slightly blue green eyes and bowed mouth. Even the little upturn of his nose was the same, and he didn't have a wrinkle in sight. How was it that he looked this perfect when mom had had grey coming in and laugh lines around her mouth? It just wasn't fair.

Ignoring his outstretched arms, I stopped in front of him arms crossed. "What are you doing here?"

He dropped his arms and just looked at me. What was he staring at? It wasn't like he hadn't seen me before. I hadn't exactly changed since the age thirteen. Yea, I had boobs now and maybe a curvier figure, but I was overall still the same.

"You didn't call me." Had his voice always been that melodic? I glared down at the ground and kicked the dirt beneath my feet.

"Didn't think you'd care."

I watched his face turn from concern into anger and then controlled irritation. Wish I had that much control over my temper. I usually just let it all out. Probably another reason why I was getting in trouble all the time.

"Of course I care, Eleanor. I'm not completely heartless."

I snorted. "Could have fooled me."

His eyes returned to their previous concern, and for a moment, he seemed flustered. "I wanted to be here for you. Especially today. I...I didn't know. I didn't see."

I stared at him for a moment, my mouth agape. I watched as he dragged a hand through his hair in a gesture I had never seen him use before. My dad was not the frazzled type. He didn't get flustered. He didn't show emotion. He definitely never said anything about ever seeing anything. My shocked look must have made him realize he was breaking his usual cool exterior, because he quickly dropped his hand and hid his eyes behind his sunglasses.

I forced my mouth closed and put on my best interrogator face. "You didn't see what exactly?"

"Don't start, Eleanor. You know damn well what I said." Oh, he wasn't as put together as he seemed. I took joy in knowing he wasn't as perfect as he put off. Meaning he could be hurt.

"Don't what? Don't wonder why my father is never around? Don't ask why he has never thought to mention to me, not once, that he could see stuff too?" I hold a finger up in his face. It felt good to vent. "Or how about the fact that when I was five, I watched my mother die and had nightmares about it for months!"

"Enough, Eleanor. Stop." The calm in his voice made my own repressed anger break its leash.

"No! You don't get to tell me when it's enough. Do you want to know she died crying out your name? Do you? She was waiting for you to save her!" I gripped the front of his meticulous suit, happy to ruin something of his. "Why? Why would she call for you? A husband who was never there, when I have been there for the last eighteen years, and she wouldn't let me save her. She wouldn't let me!" A large part of me delighted in the pain that marred my father's flawless face. I wanted him to suffer. I wanted to hurt him like he had hurt me all these years. Like he had hurt her.

"How long has your hand been bothering you?"

I took in short shallow breaths and stared at him. I released his suit jacket and stepped back, my brows drawn together. What? Out of all that, he was only worried about my scar? I looked down at my hand where I had been rubbing at it. I hadn't even realized I had been doing it.

"A few months. Why does that matter?"

I almost laughed when he cursed and pulled out his phone like nothing I just said mattered. Watching him talk into his phone, I realized something. The man I thought was my father was not who I thought he was at all. I didn't know this man.

"Yes, now. Perfect. Be there soon."

My brow furrowed as he hung up his phone and turned back to me. "What's going on? What's my scar have to do with anything?"

He suddenly grabbed me by the shoulders, and I tried not to flinch against him. My father had never touched me before, and I didn't really want to see anything about him. But nothing happened. No blurred eyes. No images. Nothing. It was almost like he didn't exist.

"We have to go."

"Go. Go where? I'm not going anywhere with you." I tried to jerk out of his grasp, but he tightened his grip, and I couldn't break free.

"I'm sorry. There's no time." He pressed his lips to my forehead in the way I'd always secretly hoped he would. When he pulled away, I could only stare at him in wonder.

"No time for what?"

But my question went unanswered as the world started to dark around me. Later, much later, I would wonder how nobody noticed when he picked me up and faded back into the trunk of the tree like he was never even there.

CHAPTER 3

SOMETIMES WHEN I dreamed, I found myself sitting in my own personal movie theater where a reel of my life played out on the screen. There was never anyone else around. Just me, in the dark, watching my life pass by.

To my utter irritation, the reel never went further than where I already was in my life. So, when the screen went dark and the reel started to click against the projector, I was left empty and hollow. Alone.

Bullshit. The whole thing was utter bullshit.

Was I not allowed to see my own future? Didn't I deserve that much? Was it God's idea of protecting me from myself? I hardly thought after everything I'd seen and felt that He would think that this would be His way of saving my sanity. From what I'd witnessed, God didn't give two shits about me or anyone else.

He was that mean girl in high school who spread rumors to other kids just to see the horror and mayhem unfold.

If it was the very fact that I was getting screwed over in the whole deal, then I could appreciate the irony. I liked irony. Like the time a bully named Reece at my middle school cut in front of the whole line just so he could get the last piece of pizza, only to find out it had pineapples on it. See, irony. Didn't want that gross crap anyway, and neither did Reece.

But I had gotten to see even Reece's death. I could see everyone else's future, but my own. In the end, I guess I was just like everyone else. Waiting in the dark for a future unwritten. I had never liked the dark. Too many shapes and whispers around the edges that fought to be free from.

"Eleanor," they whispered. Their voices were like raspy smoke victims, all crackled and harsh. "We see you, Eleanor. We're going to find you."

Usually by this point, I was curled up into a ball on the floor of my theater with the dark creeping in around me. This dream was different than the others. This time, they didn't come any closer. They were stuck. As I looked around the corners of the theater, I could feel the pressure of their struggles as they tried to get to me. Why weren't they moving?

I suddenly cried out as a burning overtook my right hand. The scar. I stared down at it and realized it wasn't like it was before. It was red and festered like an infected wound. What in world was going on?

"Help!" A scream ripped from my throat as the pain radiated through my hand, and I fell to my knees. The whispers in the dark laughed a haunting cackling that bounced off the walls.

"No one to help you now. We can see you, Nabi." The last word came out as a hiss. *Nabi.* They repeated it over and over, almost like a prayer. The sound of them grew louder and louder, until I couldn't even hear the sound of my own voice anymore.

As I knelt there with my hands over my ears, trying to drown at the noise, the burning in my hand started to fade, and with it, another voice could barely be heard over the chants.

"Eleanor."

Dad?

The chanting around me came to an abrupt halt, as if they had heard it too and were trying to listen. I lowered my hands and slowly pushed to my feet. With the pain in my hand gone, I scanned around me and saw the shadows still there, just barely moving around in the corners of the room. Were they scared of my dad?

"Wake up, Eleanor."

The sound of his voice caused light to shine into the darkened theater, and my eyelids fluttered open. Even as my consciousness awakened in the back of my mind, in the theater, I could still hear them.

No longer silent and waiting, but panicked and rushing about in the darkness. In their haste for escape, I could still catch them chanting the word.

Nabi.

"I think she's waking up now, Bart. Give her some room." My eyes snapped open at the new voice of a woman near my feet. One hand rubbed my eyes as I tried to sit up on what seemed to be a leather couch. Where was I?

"Don't move too fast, dear. Though you were out cold, shifting still makes most of us nauseous the first time." There was a slight musical note to her voice, and I wondered for a moment if she was related to my dad.

I blinked my eyes several times as I stared at the dark-haired woman at the end of the couch. She stood with her arms crossed under her breasts, which looked like they could spill out of the v-cut in her deep purple suit jacket at any moment. Was she even wearing a shirt under that thing?

"Who are you?" Damn. Even my voice sounded hollow compared to hers. Maybe I should stop smoking. Nah.

"Eleanor, don't be rude." My eyes jerked from the woman and over to my dad, who stood by my side. Hands in his pockets, he had a smug expression on his face that was just itching to be slapped off. If my hand didn't still ache, I would have done it by now.

I swung my legs over the side of the couch and took in the room around me. We were in an office. The woman's I assumed. Books filled the bookshelves that decorated the walls. A large mahogany desk took up much of the space in the middle of the room. There was no name plate and no personal items that would give away who she was.

"What did you do to me?" I was proud of the venomous tone my voice had taken on. It was hard to sound threatening when you had to look up at someone.

"Eleanor, it was for you own good." My dad didn't even remotely sound apologetic for what he'd done. "You wouldn't have left with me otherwise, and we were running out of time."

"You're damn right I wouldn't have." I stood and curled my hands into fists. I'd never had a lot of patience. As an only child, I had always gotten what I wanted, when I wanted it, and right then, I wanted answers. Ignoring the stranger in the room, I shoved a finger at my dad. "You think you can just pop back into my life whenever you want and abduct me because you think it's best? Well, listen up, pops." I popped my p aggressively. "I'm a grown ass adult. Eighteen, almost nineteen. I don't have to do anything you say. In fact, you lost that right when you left Mom and me to fend for ourselves."

I shoved around him, intent on leaving. Never mind that I had no idea where I was. I just needed to get away from him. A thin but strong hand latched onto my elbow and halted my dramatic exit. Glaring down at the black painted nails, I jerked my eyes up to the dark purple eyes of the stranger. I was startled enough by her unusual eye color to drop my scowl but what really got to me was I couldn't see her death either.

Leaning in close to her, I stared hard. "What are you?"

Her crimson colored lips tilted up on one side. "Stay and find out."

She had me there.

I contemplated for a moment between barging out of the room or satisfying my curiosity. The fact that my dad also couldn't be read was what won out. Whatever this woman was, I had little doubt my dad was too.

"Fine," I clipped, pulling my arm from her grasp. I didn't sit back down on the couch, but wandered around her room.

"Eleanor—" my dad started.

"Elle," I interrupted him, my eyes skimming the books on the shelves. *Book of Enoch. The Rise and Fall of the Morning Star. Encyclopedia of Celestial Beings.* Frowning at the books, I turned back to my dad and the strange woman. "Are you some kind of religious organization?"

My dad gave an exasperated sigh. "If you would just sit still, I can explain."

"Why don't you let me, Batariel?" The woman placed a hand on his arm in a way that was too familiar for my liking, her lips curving up at the edges.

"Very well, Azazel. You were always far better at these things." He lifted his arm, shifting his suit jacket to look at his watch. "I'm needed back anyway." They exchanged a knowing look before my dad turned his attention back to me. "I know you hate me right now, Eleanor. But please know that everything I do is to protect you. Please stay here with Azazel. She'll explain everything and protect you."

Anger boiled in my stomach, and I stepped forward to shout at him for leaving me again, but he was gone in a swath of shadows before I even took a breath to speak. Gritting my teeth together, I swiveled my rage onto the only other person in the room. Azazel.

The woman wasn't affected by my glare in the slightest. In fact, she seemed amused by it. Sashaying across the room, she reached passed me, making me flinch, but she only plucked a book from the shelf. "Since you don't seem too surprised by your father's shifting abilities, I'll spare you the 'magic is real' lecture and get right down to the thick, juicy center of things." She opened the book in her hands and flipped through some pages before plopping the book into my hands.

I stared down at the page before me. A black and white image spanned the page. Bodies with wings fell around the edges with swords in hand. Several other winged creatures swooped in from the heavens, lashing their swords out at the fallen as rays of light from the sky poured down on them. I read the underlying subtitle.

The Fall of the Angels.

I glanced up from the book to Azazel and then back down. "You can't really believe in this crap, can you? I mean, angels are cool and everything, but to really believe they exist?" I puffed a bit of air and rolled my eyes, snapping the book shut to push it back at her. "That's just crazy."

Azazel didn't even flinch at my words, her dry expression reaching all the way to her eyes. "No crazier than a girl who can see the death of everyone she touches. Except for me and of course, your father." Her lips ticked up at the edges. "At least, not yet anyway."

"What does that mean?" My brows drew together as I watched her push the book back onto the shelf where it belonged and then walk over to her desk.

Leaning against the edge of the desk, she placed her hands on either side of her. "What it means, Eleanor, is that your father and I are angels." My mouth gaped slightly at what she was saying, not because I believed her, but because of the stupidity of it all. But she didn't stop there. "And you are a Nephilim. The daughter of an angel."

I shook my head at her, wrapping my arms around myself as I stalked back and forth in front of the shelf. "That doesn't make any sense. My mother was human. She didn't have any abilities. And my dad is just an asshole." I scoffed, muttering to myself, "Angels are supposed to be of light and kindness. If Dad is an angel, God fucked up somewhere."

Listening to my rambles, Azazel laughed, a long throaty sound. "Oh, God doesn't fuck up, as you say. We are angels, but not those who reside in Heaven. At least, not anymore."

I spun around on her, my eyes scanning up and down her form. "You're a demon? Of course, you are. Makes sense," I confirmed with a jerky nod. "It sure makes more sense than being angels."

Azazel was up and off the desk in seconds, her face inches from mine as she gripped my chin in her sharp clawed hand. "Don't ever lump me or the great Batariel in with those Hell bottom feeders again."

I snorted in her face. I didn't mean to. It just happened. She said my dad was great. Right. Sure. Great at ditching his family.

Azazel jerked back from me, a look of disgust on her face. "Regardless of your belief or not, you are in need of protection, and you are lucky that I owe Batariel my life."

"What, did he save your stock portfolio?" I rolled my eyes once more and sank back down on the couch, throwing my legs over the side. I really needed a cigarette. I contemplated how pissed off Azazel would be if I lit up right there.

Ignoring my question, Azazel went to the office door and opened it. "Ayden, would you come in here?"

I sat up on the couch to watch a girl around my age walk into the room. She had hair the color of burnt coals and ember colored eyes. Her lips were colored a flaming red to go with the red of her eyeshadow. Those ember eyes found mine and narrowed in suspicion as she took me in. Well, look all you want, missy. I hadn't let someone bully me since I turned twelve.

"Yes, my liege?" Ayden peered up at Azazel with adoration and wonder.

It made me want to gag.

"Would you show Eleanor around? She will be going to school here for the time being." Azazel locked eyes with me as if she knew I was going to argue the fact.

I wasn't going to give her the satisfaction. Besides, the sooner I got out of here, the sooner I could have a nicotine fix. Jumping to my feet, I walked up to Ayden. "Cool. Nice to meet you. Let's go." Before she could respond, I walked out of the office.

CHAPTER 4

I WALKED BESIDE Ayden as she showed me the school. I used the word 'school' loosely, because the place looked more like an old castle renovated to be livable than any school I'd ever seen. Where was the stained hasn't-been-white-in-years linoleum? Where were the florescent lights and ugly blue lockers?

The main theme of this school was stone. And lots of it. Gray stones lined the walls and the floors. The only color came from some large gold framed pictures of different scenes from the Bible and even ones I'd never seen before.

Noah's Ark.

Adam and Eve in the Garden of Eden.

The Fall of the Angels, which I'd already seen in the book Azazel showed me. The others were different scenes that featured angels and demons, as well as one that had all the angels on one side and the fallen on the other side, each racing toward a singular figure in the middle wielding a sword above their head.

"That's the Watcher," Ayden said over my shoulder, making me jump in place.

I twisted around to look at her curiously. "What's a watcher?" It was the first sentence the girl had said to me since we left the office. I think she didn't like me too much. Too bad. I wasn't here to make friends. I didn't want to be here at all.

Not making fun of me for my lack of knowledge, she seemed to shift into teacher mode. "The Watcher is said to be the one who will bring about Utopia or the Apocalypse. Or whatever." She waved her hand in front of her face and grinned. "If you believe that kind of crap."

I snorted. "I don't."

"Good. So..." She trailed off as she walked back toward the center aisle. "I get the feeling you don't exactly want to be here."

I shoved my hands into my armpits and scuffed my booted foot on the ground. "What gave that away?" I was still wearing my funeral clothes. I'd have to find something else to wear soon. Though one look at Ayden's plaid skirt and white button-down shirt with crimson colored necktie, and I was thinking my mourning clothes might be the better choice.

"Believe me, I didn't want to be here either." Ayden gave me a knowing look. "Not many of us do. But we don't really have a choice. If we weren't here, the angels would kill us all."

I started at her words. "What? Why?"

Ayden gave me a confused frown. "Don't you know?"

I shrugged my answer.

Pursing her lips at my utter lack of knowledge, Ayden asked, "You do know you're a Nephilim, right?"

"Well, yeah. I got that part in there." I pointed a thumb back at Azazel's office.

"Hold on. Hold on, just one dang minute." Ayden grabbed my arm and jerked me back.

I winced against the onslaught of images that shoved their way into my head. A spear pierced through my chest, the pain so excruciating that I gasped sharply. I pulled my arm from her grasp to break the connection, stumbling back from her startled expression.

"Uh, what was that?"

I held a hand up signaling to her I needed a moment. Bent at the waist, I put my hands on my knees and heaved in deep breaths. Most of the visions I had weren't that visceral. The last one that had been this bad had been my mom. It wasn't a vision that was easy to forget.

"Don't touch me." I finally said, lifting my head. "Just don't."

"Oooh..." Ayden's eyes widened, and her mouth formed an O shape. "You're one of those. I was wondering, but I guess it makes sense given your..." She waved a hand at my clothing. "Fashion choices."

I glanced down at my dress. "Uh, I just came from a funeral, but what do you mean 'one of those'?"

Ayden's brows shot up. "Oh. Sorry. I didn't mean—"

I jerked my hand across the air. "Forget about it. Just answer the question."

"Well, first off..." Ayden shifted and then looked around. When her eyes finally settled, she pointed toward a set of double doors. "You need the whole shebang. It's not often we have a virgin amongst us."

I frowned. "Virgin? I'm not a—"

Ayden giggled. "Not that kind of virgin, but that's good to know. I don't have to walk on eggshells around you when I talk about my hookups."

Cocking a brow, I allowed Ayden to lead me toward the double doors. "So, you know you're a Nephilim, but do you know what that even means?"

I shrugged and tossed my blonde hair over my shoulder. "My douche bag dad banged my mom and made me. We're all one big freaky family." I hugged my waist as I chewed on my lower lip. I could really go for a cigarette about now.

"Yeah, yeah, but do you know what that means?" She lifted her hand and pulled on the door handle of the double doors. Like in one of those slow-motion scenes in the movies, a large hall sprawled out before me. "You're not alone."

Long tables filled with kids of all ages sat around the room. Plates and trays sat in the middle of the tables full of food for them to pick off of. Some of them read books. Others chatted with their friends. Then a scream erupted on one side where a set of twin guys about my age were laughing as wind whipped around them, building a cyclone in the middle of the table.

My eyes turned to saucers, and I looked to Ayden. Not she or anyone else was freaked out by the tornado the guys were creating. The girl who had screamed was cursing the twins out for messing her hair up, not because she was scared.

I gaped at the scene before me and then almost fainted dead away when another boy came up and shot fire out of his hands. It whirled around the top of the cyclone, almost hitting the ceiling.

"And I thought I was a freak," I muttered to myself, unable to comprehend the magnitude of what was going on in front of me.

Ayden bumped me with her arm and laughed before adding a quick, "Oops, sorry."

I waved her off with a sigh. "I'm used to it. The first time is always the hardest."

"Gotcha." Ayden nodded, leading me toward the ones making the ruckus. "I've only known one other seer before. We don't get many of your kind."

"My kind?"

She smiled as if it were something fantastic to be a rare type of freak. "Someone who's mom and dad are Nephilim." She gestured around the room. "Most of us either have one parent who is a Nephilim and one who is human. Sometimes, one parent is an actual angel and the other human, but that's pretty rare."

I frowned. "How do you know what kind I am based on my...ability?"

Ayden stopped by the group before turning to me. "That's easy because seeing the future is a power only God is supposed to have. You're technically not supposed to exist, but the fallen are far more lenient than the angels."

I let that thought swim around my head while Ayden jumped into the fray nearby. The moment the twins—both red headed and freckle faced—saw her, they dropped their arms. The dark headed guy making the fire also stopped, and the fiery cyclone dispersed into thin air.

"Hey, Ayden. What's up?" one of the twins asked, but the other one saw me over Ayden's shoulder and grinned.

"Oooh...fresh meat." He sauntered over to me and reached out. I ducked before he could throw his arm around my shoulder and backed up several steps.

Ayden caught the action. "She's a seer."

The others collectively nodded in understanding before returning to what they were doing. The guy who had tried to touch me offered me an apologetic look. "Sorry. I didn't know."

"It's fine." I held a hand up, still a bit dumbfounded by the lot of them.

"I'm Zephyr. That handsome bastard over there is my brother, Bayu." He gave me a lopsided grin. "And who might you be?"

"Elle," I quipped simply. I thought I was done with the whole school introduction stuff until I went to college. I didn't really want to meet new people if I was just going to leave again. I had enough of my own issues to deal with without adding all their deaths to my vault.

"That was a cool trick you did," I continued, making conversation. "What are you, some kind of elemental?"

"Good guess!" Ayden popped back into our conversation beaming. "I was just going to show you the different groups. We're elementals." She gestured to herself, the twins, and the other fire guy. "The twins can control wind, obviously. Joash and I both do fire."

"I'm Coral!" A pink haired girl with a pixie cut poked her head into the group. "I can control water." She swirled her hands in the air, water pooling into the shape of a horse. It neighed and jumped across the air before me. When I reached out to touch it, it splashed to the ground soaking my stockings. "Oops." The girl giggled. "I'm not that good yet."

"Normally, the elementals stick together and the mentals do the same, but since our liege assigned you to me, I think we can make an exception." Ayden grinned, proud of herself for her benevolence.

I cocked a brow at her, but then frowned and asked, "Mentals?"

The one named Joash answered, "Them lot over there." He pointed toward the opposite side of the room. Most of them weren't talking, but seemed to be staring at each other intently, while the others were flipping pages without touching them. A few of the younger ones were tossing a ball without their hands.

"You would normally be over there with your kind, being a seer and all." Zephyr patted me on the shoulder and then jerked his hand back with a wince. "Oops, sorry."

I breathed through the attack of a violent death, something that seemed to be a theme here at the school. I grasped my head and shook it. "I'm fine. Just hurts more with you guys."

"Hurts more?" Zephyr exchanged a look with the others. "I've never heard of visions hurting before."

Oh. Well. That sucked. Not wanting to talk about it anymore, I turned to Ayden. "Uh, could I see my room? I do have a room, right?"

Ayden's face brightened. "Oh, yeah. Of course. Let's go." She waved to the others and ushered me out of the room. The mentals stared at me as I walked pass them with pity in their eyes. I avoided their gazes, knowing they could see into my mind. Get a good look, because I was happy to spread the misery around.

CHAPTER 5

AYDEN DROPPED ME off at my room, telling me about the coed bathroom across the hall before leaving. The room itself wasn't much bigger than some of the dorm rooms I'd seen in the brochures Nikki and I had looked at.

Shit.

Nikki!

She must be freaking out right now. I'd totally disappeared. I patted myself and realized I didn't have pockets in this dress, and hence, no phone.

Fuck. Fuck. Fuck.

"Uh, hey, Ayden," I called out to her as she left me at my room.

"Yeah? What's up?" Ayden cocked her head to the side. "Need a map? I can come back at dinner time."

"Oh." My brows shot up. "That would be great, but I was going to ask if I could borrow your phone, or if you knew where I could get one."

Ayden frowned, walking back toward me. "Isn't it with your stuff?"

I leaned my hand on the door frame and glanced back behind me. "My stuff." She was right. There was stuff in my room. I recognized my old suitcase as well as my mom's brand-new maroon set. I could only imagine what was packed in them. The thought of someone else going through my stuff irked me in the worst way. My eyes landed on the small desk next to the twin sized bed and found my black clutch from the funeral.

I practically raced to it, not caring what I looked like to Ayden. I almost ripped off the zipper trying to get it open and sighed heavily as not only my phone, but my pack of cigarettes came pouring out. Fuck yes.

"Find it?" Ayden stood in the doorway, concern on her face.

I gave her my first genuine smile since I arrived, holding them close to my chest. "Yes. I did. Thanks." I turned my phone over in my hand and saw the missed calls and messages across the front of it. Not wanting to be a dick to my first ally there, I added on, "I'll see you at dinner?"

"Of course." Her ember eyes crinkled at the edges. "Get settled in. It's a lot to take in at once. I wouldn't blame you if you wanted to make a break for it." She winked at me before disappearing out the door.

I flipped through my notifications as I moved to close the door. No surprise, I had at least a dozen calls and text messages from Nikki. A few from my Aunt Kate, and even more from Aunt Sue. Even Uncle Bob had called me.

Knowing where my priorities were, I called Nikki back first. It rang once before Nikki's out of breath voice came through on the other side. "Oh, my fucking God, Eleanor

Marie Richmond. Where have you been? You totally disappeared from the funeral. And your aunts were freaking out having to do the lunch afterward without you. I had to actually talk them down from calling a SWAT team. Please tell me you had a normal freak out and took off for some alone time and not that you'd been abducted by some creepy funeral stalkers?"

When she finally stopped talking long enough to take a breath, I laughed into the phone. God, I loved that girl. "No. I haven't been abducted by funeral stalkers. Just my dad."

There was silence on the other line before she said, "Oh." Just oh. No judgment. No wondering what happened. Just oh. "Well, I guess that's good."

I snorted. "Good? You think my dad kidnapping me from my mom's funeral is good? One that he was late showing up to, by the way."

"You didn't call him. You can't blame him for that."

"So beside the point," I growled, continuing with my rant. "Not only did he kidnap me, but he brought me to fuck only knows where and just ditched me here."

"Have you checked maps?" Nikki asked matter-of-fact.

"Oh. No. I just got my phone. Let me look." I moved the phone from my ear and pulled up the map app. I hit the current location button and waited and waited.

Unable to find the location requested.

Of fucking course.

Putting the phone back to my ear, I snarled, "It's not working."

"Not working? Where are you? Jupiter?"

"I wouldn't rule it out," I muttered as I glanced out the long rectangle window of my stone filled room. My eyes fell to the courtyard filled with—surprise, surprise— stone statues. Long green rolling hills spread out around the black metal gate surrounding the building.

"Well, when you figure it out, call me. We have school to plan for, and I'm not letting them pair me with some rando. I need you."

I grinned at the desperation in her voice. "I love you too, Nikki. Can you tell my aunts—"

Ready to go, I crept out of my room, my head swinging one way and then the other. I half expected my dad to have set a guard up for me.

I snorted. He trusted me far too much.

Or.

He trusted Azazel to keep me here.

I shuddered. I didn't like to think of that. Who knew what that woman was capable of?

With no one there to stop me, I walked down the hallway and then the stairs Ayden had taken me up. My eyes kept track of the courtyard as I went searching for a way outside. Finally, after what felt like forever, I found a pair of double doors leading out into the fresh air.

My boots crunched on the gravel walkway as I made my way outside. There were green shrubs lined around various statues, many of them following the school's theme. Angels fighting other angels. A single angel had wings that spanned so far out, I had a hard time wondering how anyone could move the thing. The whole place was creepy in general. The creepiest were the weeping angels with their hands over their eyes, as if they were waiting for you to turn your backs on them just so they could attack.

I shivered and made sure to keep them in my line of sight. Never could be too careful.

I moved over to the gate. Briefly, I wondered if I could climb over it. Then I remembered I wasn't good at athletic things and gave up on that idea. My hand reached for the bars, but they bounced right off. Frowning, I tried again. I couldn't even touch the bars? What was this, a freaking prison?

Letting out a long groan of annoyance, I stomped back to the courtyard. Finding a good place to stand so I could keep watch, I pulled my first cigarette from my pocket. I set it between my lips and reached for my lighter…only to come up empty handed.

"No," I groaned, pursing my lips around the butt of the cigarette as I frantically searched my pockets. "No. No. I did not fucking forget it."

I pulled the cigarette from my lips and held my arms out to my sides as I screamed at the heavens, "Why? Why now? Is this all a joke to you?"

"Not particularly," a rich deep voice answered me.

"Jesus Christ." I jumped away from the voice and the person behind it, dropping my cigarette on the pathway. Black hair curled at the nape of the guy's neck. His square jaw went well with the strong nose and bow curved lips. His white tee, dark washed jeans, and black boots already put him in the not so bad category compared to all the preppy kids I'd already seen here in angel school.

"Sorry, didn't mean to startle you." The smirk on the guy's lips told me he wasn't really sorry.

"Yeah, well you did." I gave the guy a side eye as I shoved my hair behind my ear to bend down and pick my cigarette back up. Who knew when I'd be able to get more? I wasn't about to waste it on a little dirt. I looked at it longingly. The likelihood that I'd get back to my room for my lighter and back out here before Ayden came looking for me was not good.

"Need a light?"

My eyes swiveled to the guy prepared to tell him to fuck off, but the finger held out to me with a flicker of flame on the tip stopped me. I stared at it with a mixture of caution and curiosity before nodding.

Placing the butt back into my mouth, I leaned in and let the mystery guy light it. Taking a deep inhale as I moved back, I closed my eyes in pleasure. Ah. That hit the spot.

"Bad day?" the guy asked, making me crack one eye open to glance at him.

I held my cigarette in one hand and crossed my other arm underneath it. "You could say that."

"You're new here."

I rolled my eyes at his clear pick up line. "Oh, wow. You must be a mind reader. Congratulations on your astute observation." I sucked on my cigarette once more, tapping the end to shake off the ash.

The guy's lips curled up even further. "Actually, I am."

"Am what?" I arched a brow.

"A mind reader."

I cocked my head to the side. "I thought you were one of those elementals." I waved the hand holding the cigarette at him.

Crossing his arms over his well-defined chest, he mimicked my head tilt. "Can't I be both?"

I shrugged. "How should I know? Like you said, I'm new here."

We went silent for a moment. I tried to keep my mind blank. The idea that someone could peek into my mind without permission kind of rubbed me wrong. I supposed the same could be same for my ability. Not that I did it on purpose. I couldn't imagine anyone wanting to experience what I did.

"Dex."

"Huh?" I jerked my head in his direction.

"My name. You were clearly thinking what could this handsome guy's name be?" He smirked and scrubbed his hand down his jaw where a five o'clock shadow had begun.

I snorted and shook my head. "You're a horrible mind reader."

Dex took a step toward me. I took one back. "I won't bite. I just wanted to show you that you could relax."

"Why?" I stared at his outstretched hand. No way did I want to see how this hottie died. I'd like to keep him unblemished for the time being.

"I can't read your mind without touching you." He reached for me again, and I backed off once more, holding my hands up. My lit cigarette pinched between two fingers.

"No offense, but I don't touch."

He dropped his hand and frowned. "Ever?"

I took another drag of my cigarette before dropping it. I ground it beneath my boot and said, "Not if I can help it." Then I turned my back on Dex and started back toward the school.

"Hey, you didn't tell me your name."

I turned and walked backward as I smiled slightly. "No. I didn't."

"At least tell me what you are," Dex called after me once more.

I pretended not to hear him as I headed inside, muttering to myself, "I'm not sure what I am anymore."

DINNER AT THE Fallen Academy wasn't much different than in high school cafeterias. Except that the occasional outburst of magic from one student or another interrupted the otherwise normal meal.

"Not that I'm complaining, but where are the teachers?" I glanced around the dining hall, not seeing any kind of grown up person in charge around. "You know, the guard dogs?"

Joash laughed through his mouth full of potatoes. "Like they would deem us worthy enough to come down to watch us eat?"

My brows drew together in confusion.

Ayden groaned beside me. "What doofus here is trying to say is that we are being watched." She gestured around us, but I didn't see anything. "Some of the teachers are high level mentals. They don't need to be in here to know what's going on."

My mouth formed an O shape as I took in what she said. That was a bit creepy. It made it hard to think that I wasn't being watched all the time. So much for my plan to ditch this place and head back home. With my luck, Azazel would be alerted and then I'd have to deal with my dad all over again.

No, thank you.

"But don't think they're invading your privacy." Zephyr pointed his fork with a piece of chicken on the end at me. "They aren't perverts or whatever. At least, I hope not." He gave me a shit eating grin that made me think I didn't want to know what exactly he was doing in his alone time.

Ayden scowled at Zephyr. "You're just gonna freak her out now." She reached to pat me on the hand, but I withdrew it before she could touch me. She frowned but didn't comment. "What they mean is they only listen for trouble. I don't know exactly how it works, but it's not like they are listening in on your every action and thought. Believe me, no one, not even them, want that." She gave the guys a pointed look of disgust.

They laughed as if to punctuate her point.

"Did you get your class schedule yet?" Coral sat down on the opposite side of the long table between the twins. The way she gave each of them a flirty smile made me wonder if she weren't dating both of them. Or at least fantasizing about it.

I sipped from my glass of tea and nodded before scooping mash potatoes into my mouth. When Coral seemed to want a more extensive explanation, I swallowed thickly and gulped down some more tea. "Yeah, I got it. Though, I'm not sure why I need to take any of these classes. I already graduated high school. I'm supposed to go to college in the fall."

The others were quiet for a moment. They exchanged a look that I didn't understand, and then Ayden turned to me. "I know it doesn't seem like it, but it's really a good thing you're here. I was where you were a year ago. Well," she smiled softly, "I was starting my senior year, and then they came for me. If it wasn't for Azazel and the rest of the Nephilims, I don't know if I'd be here talking to you today."

"Came after you?" I frowned hard. "Who? No one's come after me."

"The angels," Bayu, the quieter of the twins, answered. "They hate us." He stabbed the meat on his plate with his knife, hatred in his eyes. "They'd kill us and our family without blinking."

I stared down at my plate, not sure how to take all this information. "I've never seen an angel aside from Azazel." And my dad, but they didn't need to know that.

"Count yourself lucky then," Ayden explained, her eyes flickering to the twins. "Some of us weren't so lucky to make it here without losing someone to them."

My stomach twisted at the thought. I had lost someone. My mom. Was she telling me that wasn't a coincidence? I wasn't the sharing type, but that didn't mean I couldn't use other ways to get my answers.

"What about your parents?" I prodded without looking too interested in the answer. "Didn't they have something to say about you being brought here? The human ones, I mean."

Coral perked up. "Oh, my mom was totally for it. She sent me to the academy when I was six. I still see her all the time. It's just safer for me here."

I glanced around the table, wondering about the rest of their stories.

"There's a mixture here. Some of us have happy beginnings like Coral. Others got here because the angels finally found them," Zephyr explained, tossing an understanding look to his brother.

My fingers caressed the mark on my hand, wondering if they had the same thing happen. "How do they find you? Do we give off some kind of beacon?"

"Not that we know of. Most of us don't exactly have powers that are easy to hide. When a kid starts fires with his hands, word tends to get around." Joash offered me a lopsided grin.

"How'd you get here?"

My head jerked to Bayu. "What?"

"Didn't you say you came from a funeral?" Ayden glanced over my clothes. "Before you changed. Which we'll need to make sure you get a uniform too. Can't have you tempting the status quo." She winked at me and giggled.

I offered her a tight smile. "Great."

"So," Zephyr prompted, continuing where his brother left off. "What's your story?" Zephyr seemed far too interested in me. I didn't do well with boys. Or men. Anyone other than Nikki, honestly. Once they found out I didn't like to be touched, they were quick to put me in the weirdo category. I had a feeling that my usual wouldn't scare this one off.

I busied myself with my food, moving the green beans on my plate from one side to the other. "Yeah. My mom died."

There was a collective inhale before an arm went around my shoulders.

"Joash, no!" Ayden cried out as my senses were overcome with the vision. My fingers dug into the side of the table as I struggled to breath. Water clogged my throat. My lungs. I couldn't scream, or even fight back. Steam filled the water around me, leaving my attacker a murky figure with long shadows spreading out around them.

I coughed and grabbed my chest, my mind thrown back into myself all at once.

"Geez, are you okay?" Coral gasped, a small sound that made me hold a hand up.

"I'm fine. Just give me—" I gasped, my throat raw and lungs still aching. "Give me a minute."

"Damn it, Joash." Ayden threw a piece of broccoli at him over me. "I told you not to touch her. She's gonna think we're a bunch of insensitive assholes."

"Which is why she should be sitting with us."

I blinked rapidly, my breathing finally coming back to normal as I slowly turned toward the new voice. A girl about mine and Ayden's age stood with two others. She wore the same uniform as Ayden, except her necktie was purple versus the red of Ayden's. I hadn't really noticed the color coordination until now. Looking around the table, I saw that each student wore a color coordinating with what their power was. Red for fire. Blue for water. I guessed brown was earth, and green for air? I didn't know how they figured that, but then again, I wasn't planning on staying long enough to find out.

The girl before me and her friends wore purple. Was that what I was going to be reduced to? A color? I didn't even like purple.

"I'm Charity. This is Bishop and Dharma." She nodded her silvery hair covered head toward the two next to her. The guy, Bishop, had black hair that hung over half of his face, hiding a stoic expression. The other girl had pale strawberry blonde hair. Her blue eyes stared into me as if she were trying to read my soul. I immediately wanted to run and hide.

"Elle." I jerked my head to her. "Why should I sit with you? Is it some rule?"

Taken back by my question, Charity's mouth dropped open before clamping shut. "No. It's just the way it is. Elementals," she gazed around the table with clear disdain, "don't understand. They have no boundaries, and will only cause you further pain. We," she gestured to her and her friends, "can help you reach your full potential, and we know a thing or two about the hazards of our abilities." She gave me a knowing look.

"Hey, we can be helpful too," Zephyr argued, his brows furrowed as he glared at Charity.

"That's so sweet," Dharma purred, her eyes locking onto Zephyr. "I'm sure she'll think that when you try to go in for a kiss and end up shooting your dirty thoughts all over her."

Zephyr's face turned beet red, his fingers curling into fists. "I would not."

"It's no use arguing with them." Ayden sighed and shook her head. "They'll be three steps ahead with anything you try to say." She turned to me. "It's up to you, Elle. I can't make you stay. And Charity is probably right." She shrugged. "I can't even begin to help you figure out your powers. I can be a friend though."

Ayden reminded me of Nikki. A less in your face Nikki, but nonetheless someone I wanted on my side.

Looking to Charity, I offered her a chilly smile. "I'll take my chances, but thank you for your concern."

Charity gaped as if she hadn't seen that coming. Apparently, they couldn't read everyone's mind, because it was clear as day that I wasn't going to go with her. I tucked that little nugget away for later.

"Come on," Charity sniffed, tossing her silvery hair over her shoulder. "She'll change her mind. They always do." She and her friends slinked away.

Turning back to my plate, I decided I wasn't hungry anymore. I pushed my plate away and stood.

"You're leaving?" Ayden's voice went up an octave. "I can't believe you're going to those crazies." She huffed and clanked her fork against her plate. "Just great."

I paused. "Chill. I'm going to my room. Not changing sides." I rolled my eyes and stuck my hand in my pocket searching for the other cigarette I'd tucked in there before. "I'm not on anyone's side. I'm on my own side."

Ayden nodded. "I get it. We all do." She jerked her head around the table, and the others copied her agreement. "You need time to adjust. Besides, tomorrow is class. You'll feel better about it then. This time next week, this will seem like the new normal." She smiled brightly. I had no plans on being here that long, but I couldn't bring myself to break her spirit just yet.

"Yeah. I'm sure you're right."

A GRIMACE MARRED my face. My nose scrunched up as I took in the uniform that had been left for me the night before. The plaid of the skirt lay spread out on the bed, the lines of it mocking me as if to say *this is your life now.*

I'd prayed to whatever god was listening for years to make my time in high school shorter. To make me suddenly smarter and able to jump grades and be out of the massive hallways crowded to the brim with adolescents. As usual, no one answered my prayers.

The rage of hormones alone set my teeth on edge, but the brush of each of my classmates against me was almost too much for me to bare. Nikki had been my only solace, and I barely had her. I was always last to leave and last to get to class, choosing to wait until the final bell had rung and the hallways were empty before making my way to my locker and then to my next class. I spent more time in detention for being late than anywhere else, but it gave me plenty of time to work on my schoolwork and less time having to worry about running into anyone after school.

It made sense that just the sight of a school uniform would bring back the anxiety of my thirteen years stuck in a death filled prison. Not that I ever had to wear a uniform, thank God for that. But I didn't see myself staying here long, and since I already had avoiding people down to a science, it shouldn't be too hard to fall back into old habits.

Or so I thought.

A knock sounded on my door.

The door opened before I could answer, and Ayden popped her flaming red head of hair into the room. "You're not dressed yet? We're going to be late for first bell." Without asking for permission, Ayden pushed into the room and shut the door behind her. She walked over to my bed and bounced down onto the mattress.

Normally, I would have thrown her out by her pleated skirt, but for some reason she reminded me of Nikki, and if I was going to get out of this place, which I hoped would be soon, I needed an ally on the inside. Better to be someone with some fire power, no pun intended, than no one at all.

"I'm always late," I commented without explanation. I grabbed the skirt and pulled it on over my pajama shorts, then shimmed the shorts out from underneath. Chunking my shirt, I slipped the white button-down shirt on over my bra and painstakingly slowly buttoned each button. When I reached for the necktie, Ayden snatched it from the bed before I could touch it.

"So, they put you in the mind squad." Ayden's lips twisted to one side as she twirled the purple tie around her finger.

I arched a brow and reached for the tie. "Why wouldn't they? My power is more mental than physical."

She jerked it out of my reach with a smirk. "I don't know. You have something about you." She glanced over me with a curious spark in her eyes. "You've got the manic-depressive thing going on, and that is totally something the mentals have down pat, but I heard you in the office the other day." Ayden pulled the tie tight between her hands just out in front of her, her amber gaze locked on mine. "You have far more rage in you than they do. Perhaps your father had a bit of fire in him as well?"

"Who knows?" Not wanting to talk about my dad, I snatched the tie from her hands before she could stop me and tossed it onto the desk. I'd probably get in trouble for not being in full uniform, but fuck them. I wanted to get kicked out anyway.

I shoved my feet into my combat boots and stalked to the door. Ayden didn't seem put off by my action, and simply followed after me with a particularly gleeful skip in her step.

"Why are you so cheerful?" I finally asked, no longer able to handle her skipping.

Ayden grinned from ear to ear, her hand coming out in front of her to bounce a little fire ball in her hand. "Oh, no reason. Just Professor Rufus is going to blow a gasket."

"Who?"

"Your first class, Intro to Enoch," she explained as we turned down a hallway and then a set of stairs. "Every new student has to take it. It's supposed to answer any and all questions we have about who we are and where we come from." She scoffed and rolled her eyes, the ball in her hand almost tumbling to the ground before she caught it. "As if one class is going to answer all of life's mysteries? Certainly not ours."

"Right."

I let her continue to rattle on until we reached my first class. Ayden had a different class to get to, but if she cared about being late, she didn't show it. Definitely, not like Nikki, who was always on time to everything. She'd be on time to her own funeral if she could. Fuck, I missed her.

After saying goodbye to Ayden, I opened the door to a classroom full of students dressed in similar outfits to mine but of all different ages. Some were closer to Ayden and my age, but others were so much younger that they barely fit in the desks they were assigned to sit in without slipping out of the bottom. A man in his mid-forties stood at the head of the class with a book in his hand. He seemed to be in mid-sentence when I entered, and paused to give me the most aggravated glare.

"And you are?" The slightly stiff tone to his voice, which only came off more annoyed laced with his British accent, made me believe Ayden had been right about him.

"Elle Richmond."

Something flickered across his face—recognition and a careful curiosity I didn't understand. He snapped the book shut and turned to me, holding the book against his waist. "Well, Miss Richmond, class starts at eight and it is now eight ten. Tell me, did you get lost? Alarm not go off? Please tell me, because I am eager to know what catastrophe has befallen you to not only be late to my class, but to not be in full uniform as well."

Wow, does this guy have a complex.

Every eye in the room settled on me, just as eager to know what I would say to their professor's condescending questions. However, I'd been up against people like him before. This wasn't my first asshole with a school backing him, and it seemed like he probably wouldn't be my last.

At my old school, I would have given them some snarky remark about meeting my dealer or getting in a gang bang between classes, anything but the truth—I didn't want to end up in a mental institute, after all—but I could be honest with Professor Rufus, and that was exactly what I did.

Adjusting the books in my hands, I stared down the crotchety man and blandly stated, "I didn't particularly feel like having a multitude of deaths shoved into my being by brushing up against every member of the student body on my first day, but if you would just let me touch you, I'd be happy to tell you how you die." I held my hand out to him, expecting him to laugh me off or give me detention, but the fear in his eyes…that was new.

"N-No. No, thank you." Clearing his throat, Professor Rufus lifted his book up once more and then nodded toward an empty seat. "Well then, let's get on with attendance. Eleanor Richmond."

I arched a brow, but then muttered "Here" before sauntering over to my chair. Sitting down, I opened my book up to the page number written on the board. While Professor Rufus finished up roll call, a boy no older than thirteen leaned toward me.

"That was fricking awesome."

I smiled. "Thanks."

"I'm Trevor." He held his pale freckled hand out toward me, his bright green eyes and dirt brown mop of hair on his head screamed earth elemental, even if the tie around his neck hadn't been the same shade of brown.

I stared at the hand for a moment, then quirked another brow at him. "Seriously?"

Trevor glanced down at his hand and then back to me, his face going shock white before flushing a deep shade of red. "Oh, yeah. Sorry."

"It's fine," I muttered, blowing out a breath of air and flicking through the pages of my book. Angels falling from heaven. God smiting them for their hubris. Lucifer taking control of the angels cast down to earth. It was all very doom and gloom. Not like I didn't have enough of that in my life.

"So, why didn't you wear your necktie?" Trevor whispered, turning back to me when Professor Rufus gave us his back. "You're a mental, right?"

I didn't know what to say to that. I guess that was what they pegged me for, but like Ayden had explained earlier, I didn't feel like one of them. Their whole it's-the-end-of-the-world-everything-has-to-be-taken-seriously vibe was so not me. Sure, my power sucked. Who wanted to know exactly how everyone around you died, let alone feel it? That didn't stop me from being the best sarcastic asshole I could be. I certainly wasn't going to be one of those five-seconds-away-from-slitting-her-own-wrists kind of girls.

I gave Trevor a flat look. "I didn't like the color."

Trevor stared at me for a long minute and then snort laughed so loud that Professor

Rufus whipped back around. "Mr. Carlton, is there something funny about the battle of the giants?"

Trevor choked on his laugh, and one of the others behind him smacked him on the back as he struggled to breath. When he finally caught his breath, Trevor shook his head. "No. Nothing funny."

"I didn't think so." Professor Rufus stared him down, his hand holding the marker he was using to write on the white board. "I would think you would have more respect for your heritage than that."

"Why?"

Every turned to stare at me. Even I was surprised that the word had come out of my mouth.

Professor Rufus almost had an aneurysm by my question. "Wha...what do you mean why?" He stepped around his desk and met my gaze for the first time since I walked into the classroom. "It is your legacy, our legacy. If we don't learn from our past, we are doomed to repeat it."

I leaned back in my chair and cocked my head to the side. "Repeat what? The giants don't exist anymore, do they? I mean," I lifted my arms out to my sides and glanced around the room, "I haven't seen any giants walking about, have you?" I huffed a laugh. "It's be a bit hard to hide that kind of thing, don't you think?"

The classroom erupted into a scatter of chuckles. Looks like at least here I was funny. My old classmates weren't that entertained by me. Though, I wouldn't have bothered to argue with the teacher like I was now. Maybe it was something about Trevor? The poor kid didn't deserve to be talked down to like that, and Professor Rufus seemed afraid of me for some reason or another.

"Well, of course not," Professor Rufus tried to bring the class back to his side. "The giants were taken out thousands of years ago, but the point of the lesson isn't about the giants. It's about not repeating the past."

"And the past being that the Nephilims grew too powerful and the angels had to put them down?" I fiddled with my pencil spinning it between my fingers. "What kind of lesson is that? Stay in your place or our mommies and daddies will give us a right spanking?" I snorted as the class chuckled once more.

Professor Rufus didn't argue with me this time. He slapped his book down onto the desk with a resounding thump. "Precisely."

The pencil flipped out of my hand and skittered across the floor. I didn't bother to go after it.

The class quieted as I leaned forward and listened to what the good teacher had to say.

"You might think you're all something special. More than human, but not quite divine." His gaze stayed steady on mine before sliding across the attentive classroom. "But the point of this lesson, as Miss Richmond has so politely pointed out, is that there are angels, real honest to God angels, who have powers beyond your wildest dreams." The whole room was in a hush as we all sat on the edge of our seats. "If you get out of line, think you are more than you actually are..." He slammed his hand down on the top of his desk, making the entire room, including myself, jump in their seat. "They will squash you like the bugs you are."

If anyone was breathing in the room, I couldn't tell. My attention was focused completely on the man at the front of the room. A bug, huh? That was a new one. I'd have to remember that for the next time I had a face to face with dear old daddy. That should be fun.

CHAPTER 8

I HAD PHYSICAL education after this class, which I skipped completely. Didn't like it in high school, wasn't going to take it now.

After an uneventful lunch, I told Ayden I had to go to the bathroom so I could have an excuse to sneak a smoke. When I came out of the bathroom, I found Charity waiting for me. I took one look at Charity and turned the opposite direction.

"Where are you going?" Charity's Mary Jane's clacked on the stone floors as she rushed to catch up with me.

I dug my hand into my bag and pulled out the cigarette I'd stashed their earlier. "To have a smoke."

"We have the next class together," Charity stated, as if that were enough to stop me.

"So?"

To my surprise, Charity grabbed my bag and jerked me to the left. "So, if you don't want to get caught and be on time, you'll go this way. They do field practice on Mondays."

I surveyed Charity. What was her deal? She didn't have her little minions with her this time, and she'd made sure to grab my bag and not my arm, which was no doubt the easier of the two. Plus, she was helping me get away with breaking the rules.

Deciding to see where this went, I jerked my head toward the hallway. "Alright then. Lead the way."

I followed Charity, acutely aware of my surroundings. It wouldn't be the first time I'd trusted the wrong person and ended up battered and bloodied behind a dumpster. Evidently though, I wasn't the only student who needed their nicotine fix. Or their high, if the scent in the air was anything to go by.

Charity brought us out a side door into a small courtyard hidden between two stone buildings. A handful of students all around my age leaned against the walls and slouched on the ground. Some of them wore the purple necktie and others didn't. It seemed the so called them versus us line Ayden and Charity had drawn at dinner didn't apply to this place.

"Come on," Charity took a joint from one of her purple neck tied friends and inhaled deeply. "We only have about fifteen minutes before the hallway rounds come by again."

She didn't have to tell me twice. I shoved the butt of my cigarette in between my lips and flicked the lighter I'd made sure to remember this time.

Taking a deep inhale, I scanned the little hidden alcove and harrumphed.

"What?" Charity arched a brow, taking another drag of her joint before passing it back to her friend.

I shook my head and laughed. "Nothing. Just didn't expect this is all."

She smirked. "You think that since we're Nephilim we're not also teenagers? We still drink. We smoke. We fuck. Just because we have holy blood doesn't mean we're not still part human. Besides..." She glanced away from me and stared off into the distance. "If any of us have a right to need an escape, it's us. You know?"

I flicked the end of my cigarette and nodded. "Yeah. Right."

We stood there in not so awkward silence, filling our lungs and heads with anything but what we were and what this life meant we had to be. No one moved until an alarm went off, making everyone jump.

"Relax." The guy Charity had been sharing a smoke with pulled his phone out and hit a button on the side. "It's the five-minute warning alarm. We better clear out of here." He exchanged a look with a Charity, who nodded and kissed him on the lips.

She walked past me and held the door open. "Come on, we have one more class before lunch break, and this one, you won't want to miss."

Taking a final drag of my cigarette, I tossed it on the ground before stubbing it out with my boot. I blew the smoke out the side of my mouth as I followed her inside.

"Why are you being so nice today?" I finally couldn't hold the question back.

Charity gave me a sideways look. "What do you mean? I wasn't being mean at dinner. I was stating facts."

I rolled my eyes. "You say po-tay-toh, I say po-tah-to." When Charity gave me a confused frown, I elaborated. "You were being kind of a bitch. I should know. It's kind of my thing."

"Oh."

She didn't say anything else about the matter as she led me through the hallways, taking paths I would never have thought to take, but it kept me from bumping into anyone on the way to our next class. When we reached the door, she stopped me with a hand once more on my bag and not my body.

"You don't have to keep your guard up so much here. Just so you know." She locked eyes with me, her face full of understanding. "We won't call you a freak or beat the shit out of you for being different. And believe me," Charity crossed her arms over her blouse and glanced down at the ground, "we all have our defense mechanisms to keep people at arm's length. I'm sure the others told you we didn't all come here at birth."

"Yeah. So, I've heard."

Her gaze lifted from the ground, and a small smile played on her lips. "So, don't be so hard on yourself. The world already does that, no reason for us to add to the burden."

I found myself smiling back at her as I nodded. "Got it."

Letting Charity walk into the classroom first, I scanned the room slowly. This one wasn't anything like the last classroom where the desks were organized in neat little rows. There weren't even any desks. Cushions lay about the room, and yoga mats were piled off to one side. My brows drew down as everyone began to take a seat. Charity offered me the cushion next to her, and I gratefully took it. Her minions—friends—Dharma and Bishop took the seats next to us.

The bell rang just as a familiar tall, dark, and handsome man came into the room. His head was down, reading something on his phone as he walked, so he hadn't noticed me yet. I took that moment to check him over.

His clothing was much different than the first time we met. Charcoal colored slacks covered his long legs, and a dark blue sweater stretched across the muscles of his chest. The V-neck of the sweater showed off a hint of the dark curls on his chest, and a sexy scruffy of hair decorated the expansion of his jaw.

Dex paced the front of the room, enraptured in whatever it was he was reading and not paying much attention to the class. Though, the way he held himself above the others told me this guy was a teacher.

Anyone else, and they'd have been worried that their teacher had not only seen them smoking on campus, but had also helped them light the damn cigarette. Not me. If I had plans to stay, then I might have been a little concerned. More for the fact that the sexy mystery guy Dex was my teacher than being caught smoking. I so couldn't be getting hot and bothered for the administration.

When those long dark lashes flickered up from his phone and around the room, they promptly landed on me. His brows furrowed and confusion pinched his forehead before those delectable lips pressed tightly into a frown.

"You must be Eleanor."

It wasn't a question. The tightness of his words clearly stated he wasn't happy about it.

"Elle," I corrected him, not letting him think seeing him here affected me. It didn't. Not in the least.

"Very well." He nodded and then turned to the rest of the class, our moment over and done with on all accounts. "We will be practicing memory retrieval today. It is a delicate process that requires concentration and complete control of your abilities."

The others in the room murmured with excitement.

Except me.

I didn't know how to do that. I couldn't do that. That wasn't even in the realm of my abilities. Why was I even in this class?

"Partner up with the person next to you," Dex continued, not giving me the chance to interrupt. "You will hold hands, since touch is essential for this to work, and then take turns pulling a memory. A single memory from their head." He gave the students a lopsided smile that made something in me tingle. "And be kind. No embarrassing caught-with-your-pants-down kind." He waved a hand carelessly in front of him. "And go."

Bishop turned and grabbed Charity's hands before I had the chance to pick her, leaving me with no other choice than Dharma. Not that I could, since I couldn't do this. My powers didn't go that far, and I certainly wasn't about to let someone I didn't know poke around in my brain. I thought of all those memories of death and pain buried deep in the metal box in the back of my brain. It was too big of a temptation for anyone to be faced with, let alone this girl who had a weird sort of eagerness to her face as she held her hands out to me.

I stared down at them. "I'm not touching your hands."

"Why not?" Dharma asked, cocking her head to the side dreamily. "Afraid of what I might find?"

"Not for me, for you."

"What's the problem here?" A shadow fell over the two of us, and the rest of the class quieted to see what the commotion was about.

"She won't do the assignment," Dharma told Dex, throwing me completely under the proverbially bus.

I glared at her. "Not won't. Can't." My eyes jerked to Dex's. "I'm not that kind of mental." I struggled with an explanation. "I can't read minds." I waved a hand at the others in the room. "Move things without touching them. That's not what I do."

Dex squatted down next to the two of us and fixed his gaze on me. "Azazel believes you belong be in this class. Are you what she claims you are, or do you want to tell her that she's wrong?" There was a hint of accusation in there that had nothing to do with the class and everything to do with our little encounter in the courtyard the other day.

I gritted my teeth, and, knowing I wouldn't get anywhere with that boobed up bitch, I snapped, "Fine. Let's do this."

"Good." Dex stood and walked a short way away, but I could still feel his eyes on us.

Locking eyes with Dharma, I slapped my hands into hers, flinching against the pain of her death. Wings. Feathers. Swords and spears. Just like all the others. If I'd learned anything from Professor Rufus today, it was that history had a way of repeating itself, and it seemed that the Nephilim in this school were just a few short years away from that very lesson becoming real.

DHARMA SEEMED A bit less eager to get into my mind than before. Good. She should be.

The fact that she was probably going to poke around where she wasn't wanted was bad enough. Now that I had her death in my mind, she just very well might find out more than she bargained for. To be fair, it would all be on Dex and Azazel to blame.

Dex for being a dick.

Azazel for thinking she knew best when she didn't really know me at all. Neither did my dad for that matter, but they were about to find out very soon.

But first…

"Think of a single memory in your mind." Dex's voice went over the room, instructing us but keeping his focus on me. The touch of his gaze caused an itch between my shoulders. Something I couldn't shake, no matter how much I tried.

"The more you narrow down the memories, the easier it will be for your partner to extract it from you."

"What exactly are we supposed to be doing with them once we have them?" asked a student near Dex's looming form.

His lips quirked up at the question. "Don't worry about that today. This is just practice. None of you will actually be able to accomplish the task just yet."

"But what if they do?" I couldn't help but prod. A part of me was happily giddy at the annoyance that covered his face.

"You won't."

"But what if they do?" I countered once more. "Shouldn't they know what to do with it before we get to that point? I mean, I don't want my memory just dancing around in her brain for the rest of time."

"Gah, no." Dharma made a disgusted face.

"My point exactly."

Dex rubbed his face and clenched his jaw. "*If* you are able to successfully extract a memory, the memory will be transferred to this." He held up a small clear box with an ornate clip keeping it closed. "These are memory boxes."

The class giggled.

"Not those ridiculous ones that humans make filled with junk." Dex held the box in his hand, showing it around the room. "It is made out of glass from the silver city itself. Nothing can break it, and *no one* but the owner can open it." His eyes landed on me as he finished.

Ignoring his look, I turned back to Dharma. "Don't go poking around. You won't enjoy what you see. Stick with the fluffy memory I'm going to bring to the front."

Dharma's hands squeezed mine, her gaze narrowing. "I don't need your help. Just relax and let me in."

I snorted as she closed her eyes. "That's what they all say."

"What?" Dharma's eyes snapped back open.

"Nothing."

Sighing with reluctance, I closed my eyes and brought forward a memory that wouldn't scar poor Dharma for life. Not anymore than it did me, in any case.

The memory I chose was one of the only birthdays from my childhood that I enjoyed. It was a bit hard to have birthday parties when none of the other students wanted anything to do with you. Nikki hardly counted for a full house, as much as I loved her to hell and back.

My mom had rented out the carousel for an hour for me and my friends. Except the only person who showed up was Nikki and me. So, we rode the carousel for the whole hour just the three of us. Over and over again, just so my mom felt like she got her money's worth. I barfed up all the cake I'd eaten right before hand too. All over the pretty brown horse I'd chosen and the floor beneath. My mom rushed to my side and ended up slipping in my mess, making her feet fly up in the air in the most hilarious manner.

"Wow, your family is so fucked up," Dharma commented.

My eyes flipped open to glare at the disgusted look on her face. "Screw you."

"Shh, I'm trying to concentrate."

Lifting my gaze to the ceiling, I huffed and closed them once more. I pushed the memory back to the front of my mind, feeling a little tingle, an itch really, in the back of my brain.

Something was wrong.

Dharma wasn't going for the memory I'd provided for her. I didn't know much of anything about psychic abilities, but shouldn't she have come in closer to the memory? Why do I feel her in the back of my mind and far too close for comfort to the metal box?

"What are you doing?" I tried to pull my hands away from her, but Dharma dug her nails into my skin, keeping me from wrenching my hands away and breaking her connection.

"Just relax." Dharma pushed further inside, and this time, that little itch was more of a twang. "I'm almost there."

"Stop it." I tried to envision a wall, forcing it up between the metal box and Dharma's mind. But no matter how many walls I put up, the tiresome bitch kept getting through. Out of all the mentals I'd met, I would not have pegged Dharma as the one with the real power. In any case, that real power was about to bite off more than she could chew.

"I'm warning you," I bit out, fighting against the prodding. It was giving me a headache, and I was losing ground fast.

"Almost there," Dharma murmured, not even paying attention to my threats.

"You're going to regret this," I told her before finally giving her exactly what she wanted. I relaxed.

"There we go," Dharma cooed, her mind waltzing into the depths of my mind and caressing the metal box. She tapped the locks and demanded, "Open it."

My lips ticked up. "Fine."

If Dharma had been smart, she would have realized that I was letting her into my mind far too easily. That the secrets she was trying to get her greedy little hands were being hand delivered.

The chains fell, and the door creaked open. I braced myself for the onslaught of images and feelings that were about to pour out. Poor Dharma didn't have a chance.

Her screams filled the room. The hands that had latched onto me tried to pry themselves away, but I held on tight. In the distance, through the roar of the screams and cries of pain and terror, I could hear someone calling our names. A hand on my shoulder only brought a new image. A new death to the downpour that rushed right into Dharma.

"Eleanor." A deep penetrating voice reached through the noise. "Elle. Let go."

My head angled to the side toward the sound. Then a warm coarse hand touched the back of my hand. I braced myself for the next onslaught of pain, but the sensations going through my body caused an unexpected moan of pleasure. Lips captured mine. Fingers trailed along my skin, leaving hot rivets of need in their place. A gasp ripped from my throat, startling me so much that I released Dharma's hands.

My eyes flew open and met Dex's dark brown eyes. I swallowed thickly and backed away from him and the sight of Dharma whimpering on the floor, her eyes squeezed tightly closed.

"What happened, Elle?" Dex tried to reach for me. I flinched back and scrambled to my feet.

I took in the looks of horror and terror on those who had claimed I could relax with them. That I was one of them. I was home now. No need to worry.

Fuck that.

No one was like me.

"I...I have to go." I left my bag where it was and darted out of the room, letting the door slam behind me.

Dex shouted after me, but didn't chase me down.

With classes still in session, I didn't have any issues avoiding people. The hallways were empty as I raced down them. The only sound in my ears was the pounding of my heart and my combat boots beating the ugly blue carpet spread out beneath my feet. I didn't know where I was going. I didn't know what had happened exactly.

One moment, I was giving Dharma exactly what she was asking for, and the next, I was having the most amazing experience of my life. I paused in the hallway, leaning against the wall as I breathed in and out slowly.

My hands traced my neck. I could almost still feel the touch of his lips against my skin. Dex's fingers brushing along my bare flesh, and heat pooling in my core.

What the actual fuck?

I'd never had a vision that didn't include someone dying. To have one of a sexual nature? How? Why?

All important questions, but they didn't overshadow the fact that I'd practically melted Dharma's brain. I'd wanted to teach her a lesson. Give her exactly what she wanted, but I never meant for it to go that far. I guess I was the only one who could really handle that kind of blood and carnage on the reg.

What the hell had I been thinking?

I should have left as soon as I got here. I didn't need this Percy Jackson Harry Potter hell hole. I was missing dorm room set up with Nikki. I didn't have time to play whatever *this* place was. My dad would just have to get over the fact that I was a big girl and could take care of myself, because I was not staying here a moment longer.

Pushing up off the wall, I started navigating through the massive halls back to my room. I needed to get my phone and my purse at least. I'd hate to leave all my clothes behind, but I couldn't very well bring them with me. I had to travel light. It was going to be hard enough trying to figure out how to get past the barrier that enclosed the school, but they had to open it at some point to let deliveries in and out. I just had to be patient and wait.

Rounding the corner to my room, the sight of Azazel waiting by my door brought me to abrupt halt. Damn it.

"Miss Richmond." Azazel hummed, lacing her fingers together in front of her. She was once more wearing one a suit, this one black, and thankfully, she was wearing a shirt beneath it—or rather, a vest, but still a step up.

"Ugh." I tried to walk around her, but she stepped into my path. "I'm leaving."

"Now, you know I can't let you do that." Azazel clucked her tongue and crossed her arms in front of her chest. "Your father entrusted me to protect you, and I'm not about to be the one that brings Batariel back here looking for someone to blame when his precious daughter gets squashed like the bug she is."

She reached out to brush a strand of hair away from my face, and I jerked away from her touch. I'd had enough death and pain for the day.

"I'm not a bug." I gritted my teeth and glowered. "Nor will I be kept prisoner." I stepped closer to her until we were nose to nose with each other, thankful for my high boots. "You don't know me. My father doesn't know me. Don't pretend that you do. This whole we're all in this together bullshit you're selling here? It's. Not. Me."

Azazel stared me down for what felt like forever before a broad smile slipped over her face. "Well, then. Perhaps we should find something that's a little more...you."

She turned on her heel and walked down the hallway. When I didn't follow, she glanced over her shoulder. "Are you coming? Or not?"

Fuck my life. I needed a cigarette.

C H A P T E R

AZAZEL SILENTLY LED me to a part of the school which was more worn and less inhabited by the students who were likely to make their presence known, even while in classes.

They hadn't bothered to glam up this part of the school. The walls were bare, and there weren't fluffed up chairs or oriental rugs on the floor. It was as if no one ever came down this way. Or maybe they just didn't care about that kind of stuff.

"Are you going to tell me where we're going or keep me in suspense?" I wrapped my arms around my waist and stared at the back of Azazel's head. I thought angels were supposed to have wings. But neither Azazel nor my father had any. At least, not that I could see. Were they metaphysical in nature? More of the energy variety than actual literal wings? Either way, the whole angels and Nephilim thing was still hard to wrap my brain around.

"Even with angelic blood in your veins, you are still so human," Azazel commented wistfully.

"And that's a bad thing?"

Azazel angled her head toward me, her lips ticking up at the edges. "On the contrary, we here at the Fallen Academy believe your humanity is what makes you an indispensable part of our hierarchy."

I snorted. "I thought we were nothing but bugs to be stepped on when we get out of line."

She threw her head back and laughed. "That too."

Grunting in the back of my throat, I dropped my arms to my sides as I paused in the hallway. "So, we only matter when you want something from us, is that it?"

Azazel stopped and twisted toward me. "Precisely."

"That's seriously fucked up."

My words didn't offend Azazel. She walked the few steps toward me, trying to use her presence to loom over me. "Never forget that you exist solely by our will. If you leave this place, you will be smote down by those all so holy angels the humans pray to. You are an abomination to them, but to us..." She reached out and caressed the air next to my face, not touching me. "To us, you can be something more."

It hurt my pride to step back from her, but I did it. She made my skin crawl, even without the physical touch. The fact that she had kept herself from touching me alone made me not trust her. Now that I knew what their end game for all of us was here, I trusted her even less. Not that there was much trust there to begin with. Anyone who befriended my father already had a place on my shit list.

"What if we don't want to be a part of your plan?" I countered, seeing how far I could push her before she showed her ugly side.

Azazel smirked. "You are under the impression that you have a choice in the matter? You, in the long run, do not matter. There are hundreds of children just like you who would love nothing more than to be part of the grand plan."

I flicked my hair over my shoulder and snarled, "Then get one of them to play your games." I spun on my heel, ready to make a rapid exit and continue with my plan of escape, but Azazel tempted me once more.

"The seer is waiting for us. We shouldn't keep her waiting."

I half turned back. "Seer? You mean, someone like me?"

"Did you think you were the only one?" She arched a brow and swept her arm out to the side. "It's not much further."

Already regretting following her rather than trying my luck at getting out of there, I took the few steps needed to catch up to her. "This better be worth it. I'm getting tired of your games."

Azazel shook her head and laughed as she stopped before a wooden door with black metal lining the edges and handle. "You are so much like Batariel."

My jaw clenched tight. "I'm nothing like him."

Azazel gave me a knowing look before turning on her heel and disappearing into the shadows, leaving me at the doorway with no explanation.

Like my dad? Pfft. No fucking way. I didn't abandon my family. I didn't put work above all else. I didn't...ugh. Why did I let her get me so worked up? I'd finally gotten myself to the place where I didn't give two shits about the man, and now, he just kept getting brought back up again.

And for what?

He wasn't going to change.

Kidnapping me from Mom's funeral for some kind of unconfirmed threat wasn't winning him any points from me. As far as I could tell, he was still just looking out for himself. After all, he dumped me off here and took off again. He couldn't even be bothered to explain what the hell was going on himself.

"Are you going to wait outside my door all day? The tea is getting cold."

The door had cracked open while I was having my internal hissy fit. A grey-haired woman with stormy grey eyes peeked out of the door at me.

"Oh, sorry." I shifted out of the way so she could open the door completely. I brushed passed her, noticing how much she did not scream seer. She wore a fuzzy pink sweater over a pale blue house dress with little white flowers decorating it. Her cream-colored slippers had seen better days. She seemed more like someone's grandmother than some mystical being who would know what I was going through.

"Please come, have a seat." She ushered me to a small table with a pretty white lace tablecloth. A tea pot with a yellow daisy painted on the side of it sat in the middle of the table. I slid into the chair before one of the teacups, noticing how there was only two cups. Had she known Azazel wouldn't be joining us?

If she was a seer, then probably.

"Tea?" She sat down across from me and lifted the pot up with a quirk of her brow.

I didn't actually care for the stuff, but didn't want to be rude. Get more flies with honey and all that. Or in this case, answers.

"Yes, please." I picked the saucer and cup up, holding it steady while she poured the tea.

"Sugar? Cream?"

I waved her off, settling to sip the vile bitter leaf water in silence.

The woman filled her own cup with tea and then piled in more sugar than was probably healthy for someone her age and only a dash of cream. "So...why don't you tell me about yourself?"

I gaped at her. "Uh, don't you already know?"

She laughed jovially and then sipped from her cup. Once she put her cup back down and swallowed, she leveled a look at me. "I could look into your past, your future, even your present, but I find it quite rude, don't you?"

I ducked my head down, staring at the dark liquid in my cup. "Yeah. I suppose so."

"Well, then we are in agreement. Introductions are best to start, don't you think?" She waited for me to answer as she brought her cup up to her mouth.

"Elle."

"Ah, yes. Batariel's daughter." When I flinched at my father's name, she smiled. "We can get back to him in a moment. I am Sarah." My brows rose, and she laughed. "Yes, I know. Quite the boring Biblical name. I'm sure you were expecting something far more exotic like Camilla or Lucia. Both of whom are quite lovely ladies, so you know. They work down in the kitchens."

"Oh." I didn't know what to say to that. Sarah seemed to know what I was thinking before I even said it, but she wasn't a mind reader. Perhaps it was part of her abilities? It was odd. I was used to being the one who knew things about others that could be used against them. Now I was on the opposite end of the table, and I found myself unsettled.

"I really like your...room." I glanced around the cozy area, searching for something to say to break the tension. After a long look at her collection of porcelain clowns, I wished I'd kept my mouth shut.

And people called me weird.

Sarah simply took it all in stride, laughing as she watched me struggle to keep my expression pleasant. "You needn't pretend with me, Elle. Our gift is not the easiest one to live with."

I drank deeply of my tea, grimacing against the bitter taste but preferring it to talking about my gift.

"It's my understanding that you didn't come here of your own volition."

I snorted. "You could say that."

"Hmm." Sarah stared at me for a long moment, then her eyes dipped to my hand, the one with the scar. "Your mother and father tried extremely hard to keep you hidden. It's a pity she had to die. She was a lovely woman."

I almost dropped my teacup. "You knew my mother."

Sarah smiled behind her teacup. "Oh yes, she was one of my favorite students. For a time. A rare thing indeed for an angel to bed a Nephilim, let alone marry one. Your mother was indeed special."

Dad had implied that mom was one of us—a Nephilim—but I hadn't believed him. Never in all my life did my mom ever use a power, at least not to my knowledge. To hear someone else that wasn't him confirm my mom wasn't who I thought she was gave me a sense of relief and anger.

They'd lied to me. My whole life, I thought I was the only one with my abilities. My powers. Not only was there a whole school full of kids just like me, but my own mother. My mom was one too.

I'd expected that kind of betrayal from my dad, but from her?

My eyes burned against my will, and I pushed at the emotions billowing up, not wanting to cry in front of this complete stranger.

"Don't be too hard on your mother, dear." Sarah sat her cup down and shifted it on the saucer. "She gave up using her powers to keep you safe. She believed that she could keep you hidden as long as too much attention wasn't drawn to you."

"But it didn't help," I practically bit out. "She didn't use her powers, and they still found me and killed her for it."

"Yes, that is unfortunate." Sarah nodded in agreement. "I wish I could tell you that you'd never lose another person you loved.

That this was the extent of your suffering but..." She sighed heavily and picked up the tea pot once more. " I'm afraid we are at war, and we have been for over a millennium. It will take something of great power to shift the balance one way or the other to stop it."

"What's that got to do with me?" I didn't even pretend to drink my tea anymore, pushing it away from me with a frown.

"Nothing...yet. But didn't you come here to talk about something else?" Sarah arched a white brow. "You aren't happy with Azazel's choice in classes for you?"

I crossed my arms over my chest and slouched back in my chair. "I'm not like them. I can't read minds. Or move things across the room. I don't have that kind of power. I just see things."

"What kind of things?"

"Not the kind of things anyone would want to see," I muttered, reluctant to talk about it.

"I see."

"Azazel," I started, and then paused. "She called you a seer. So, you're like me?"

Sarah smiled kindly. "Alike, but not the same. I need assistance to see the future, but you..." She stirred the milk and sugar into her tea. "You are so much more."

I scoffed, tired of being referred to a bug in one sentence and then indispensable in the other. "I'm nothing special."

"But you are," she insisted, lifting her cup to her lips to blow on it. "You have a gift. You can see all that happens before it even happens. Can change what others cannot. That's far greater a gift than any of the other mind reading or fire bending idiots can do in this school."

"But I can't!" I shook my head, straightening up in my chair. "Don't you understand? I only see death. And no one can change that." I lowered my head, moving it from side to side sadly. "Believe me, I've tried."

A hand settled over my head, and for once, I wasn't assaulted with a violent death. Sarah laid peaceful in her bed, a cup of tea on the nightstand and her beloved figurines all around her. She smiled up to the heavens, a tear sliding down her cheek as her final breath released between her lips.

"Death is inevitable." Sarah's voice soothed me as much as the peacefulness of her death. "Sometimes, you are not meant to change it, but to be the one to endure it."

I lifted my head and peered into her gentle eyes. "I can't even see my own future, how am I supposed to save anyone else's?"

"We aren't meant to see our own future, not even you." Sarah patted me on the hand and offered me a tissue.

It was then that I realized the tears I'd been fighting had fallen. When had that happened?

I took the tissue with a thank you. "I still don't see why I was put in that class. I'm not like them. I probably screwed Dharma for life."

"I wouldn't worry so much about that," Sarah explained. "She's far more resilient than you'd think. Even if she tends to bite off more than she can chew." She winked, causing me to laugh as I blew my nose.

"There's one more thing before you go." Sarah sat her cup to the side and reached for my hand. I would usually pull away, even though I'd seen her death already, but there was something about her that made me want to trust her.

"The mark on your hand." Sarah tapped on it with her thumb. "While it was given by your father, it will fade, and with it, the cap on your powers."

I frowned deeply at that. "The cap on my powers?"

She held my hand tightly, not answering my question as her eyes stared off into nothing. When her gaze finally cleared, she shook her head disappointingly. "I fear even I cannot see the extent of your abilities. Be careful."

WHILE LEAVING SARAH'S, my stomach rumbled. It was no wonder I was hungry. It was well past lunch time, and I hadn't eaten breakfast.

"Better hurry to the kitchens before they close for dinner prep." Sarah quickly explained how to get to the kitchens from her room before handing me a small stack of books.

"What's this?" I eyed the pile suspiciously.

Smiling in amusement, Sarah wrapped her sweater tighter around her shoulders. "While you're more than just a seer like myself, you'd do well to read up on our abilities. It might just come in handy later." With no further explanation, she waved me off and shut the door.

I let out a disgruntled sigh, holding the books under one arm.

Great. More homework.

Not that I wasn't grateful for her insight. I'd always been on the outside looking in, so it wasn't too surprising to be in the same place I'd always been. Still, it would have been nice to fit somewhere.

Oh well.

My stomach yelled at me again, reminding me once more to feed it.

Turning from Sarah's door, I tried to remember the directions she'd given me. I wasn't sure what time it was or if classes were close to being over. I hoped I didn't run into anyone from the last class. Or anyone in general really. Who knew how fast gossip like that spread here? If it was anything like my old school, everyone in the whole building already knew what I did.

On edge the entire walk back, I kept looking over my shoulder for someone to pop out and scream "Freak!" before demanding I leave. Not that it wouldn't be a favor to me. I'd be doubling down on a way out of here soon before they bring the pitchforks to drive me out.

To my relief, only a few people were wandering the halls, and they didn't give me more than a second glance before hurrying on their way. Maybe the news hadn't gotten to everyone yet then?

I counted myself lucky for once and made it to the kitchens. Pushing the door open, the banging of pots and pans followed by a growl of annoyance filled my ears.

"How many times must I tell you? Simmer, not boil!" yelled a man in a white chef's coat with a red bandana around his head at a poor worker. "It's not that hard." He shook his head and turned from the shaking guy. "I swear, they let anyone into culinary school these days."

Wiping his hands on a nearby towel, the man stopped when he spotted me. His eyes narrowed as he placed his hands on his hips. "The kitchen is reserved for staff only. You should eat when the other students do, or you're tough out of luck."

What kind of fucked up rule was that? I almost argued back at him, but his eyes landed on the books in my hands, and his entire expression changed.

"Oh." The word was a bell like sound that filled his whole face with glee. "You're one of Sarah's. Why didn't you say so? I'm Vinny."

Cause the grumpy bastard didn't give me the chance. And what was all this Sarah's bull crap? While I didn't belong to anyone, I was my own woman after all, I wasn't about to correct him and get booted from the kitchen. Food was a higher priority than my pride.

"Yeah, that's right." I held the books up so he could see the covers. "We got a little carried away, and I missed lunch. Would it be alright? I mean, Sarah told me..."

"Oh yes!" The man waved me into the kitchen, but like so many already, didn't touch me. I guess I wasn't the only one with a reputation. "Please have a seat, and I'll whip you up a cold plate." He paused and swung back around to me. "Or would you rather have something hot? I know the visions can be draining, but I've never been told if the temperature of the food really mattered in the way of recharging?"

I had no idea what he was talking about, since I'd never felt anything but annoyed by my visions, so I simply shrugged. "Cold is fine."

Humming along to himself and walking straight through anyone who didn't get out of his way, Vinny went about making me a sandwich, and every once in a while, would ask me about my preferences. When finished, he handed me a plate full to the brim of chips, vegetables, and the biggest sandwich I'd ever seen.

"There you go, darling. Don't hesitate to come back if you ever need an energy boost." He wiggled his fingers after me, but the second the kitchen door closed behind me, he was yelling at someone else.

Geez.

Too tempted by the plate in my hands, I snagged a pickle and munched on it as I walked back to my room.

God all mighty! I moaned my delight. If this was the way being one of Sarah's were treated, then I'd be glad to put on a collar, ball gag, the whole works, just for one of these juicy pickles.

Happily eating away at my plate, I didn't notice any of the students piling into the hallways until I was back where my room was located.

"Elle, there you are!" Ayden and Coral appeared by my bedroom door. "Where have you been?"

I held the plate up, as if it must be obvious.

Coral's pale pink brows bunched together. "How'd you get food between meals? We never get anything when we go."

"Vinny is a right dick," Ayden said, agreeing with Coral.

I lifted my other hand hold the stack of books and they both oh'd.

"Go figures. Vinny is uber superstitious. He never yells at the seers. Afraid it'll change something in his future." Ayden nodded with understanding.

"Did you need something?" I bit into a chip, savoring its salty goodness while I waited. I hoped they hadn't come here to ridicule me about what happened to

Dharma. I really didn't want to deal with that right now.

"Oh!" Ayden smiled as if remembering something pleasant. "I just wanted to tell you to stay up past bedtime tonight."

I arched a brow. "Okaaay. Why am I doing this?" It better not be some silly school prank like filling someone's bedroom with maple syrup.

Coral clapped her hands with glee. "We're going to—"

"Shhh." Ayden smacked her on the arm with a frown. "You're going to get us in trouble." Once she was sure no one was listening into the conversation, she leaned in and, with a mischievous gleam in her eyes, whispered, "I don't want to spoil the surprise. It's a once in a lifetime experience."

"Oh, really?" I continued to chew on a celery stick as I waited for her to get to the good part. I wasn't quite sure our definitions of 'once in a lifetime' were the same and needed a bit more to get my juices flowing the way theirs were. They'd been drinking some kind of Kool-Aid, that's for sure.

"For real!" Coral squealed, getting shushed again by Ayden. "No. I mean it.

We're only able to do this kind of stuff once every few years because our liege rarely ever leaves campus."

This perked my interest. Azazel left campus? Why?

"So why does it matter if she's here or not? The other teachers are still here though, right?"

Coral opened her mouth, no doubt to squeal again, but Adyen shot her a look. She pressed her lips tightly shut and bounced in place.

"None of them are always watching like Azazel," Ayden began, but then Coral jumped in.

"And Sarah doesn't give a flying flip if we go past the barrier, as long as we're careful." Coral grinned from ear to ear as Adyen glowered at her.

I busied myself eating so they wouldn't see my reaction to Coral's words. Go past the barrier? I definitely had to go now.

"Anyway, just be ready. I'll come get you at lights out." Ayden gave Coral one last warning look before they walked away.

Munching on a carrot while I mulled over what they'd told me, I ducked into my room and shut the door. I sat the plate and books on my desk and flopped down in the chair. Throwing my boots up on the edge of my desk, I popped open one of the first books on the pile.

I couldn't focus on the words though. My mind kept going back to Ayden and Coral.

They hadn't asked about Dharma. They hadn't even seemed scared of me. Did the school cover it up? Or was it not as bad as I thought it was?

The sight of Dharma sprawled on the floor her eyes with staring at nothing made me shudder. Nope. Definitely not over exaggerating.

I ate about half of the massive sandwich Vinny made me before my phone rang.

Thank all that was good and sarcastic. It was Nikki.

"Have my aunts driven you insane yet?"

Nikki scoffed. "Yeah right. I'm Jewish, remember? My mom has guilt down to an art. There is no way they're gonna break me." I chuckled over her words, slipping out of my chair and over to my purse. As I dug around inside, Nikki asked, "Have you figured out where you are yet?"

"Not yet, unfortunately, but I have a..." I mumbled under my breath as I tried to find my spare lighter. I'd left my bag in class and hadn't had a chance to go get it yet. That wasn't going to stop me from lighting up though. "Ah ha!" My fingers wrapped around the lighter, and I snagged a cigarette from the pack and took up a seat by the window.

"What was that 'ah ha' about?" Nikki prodded. I could hear the frown on her face.

"Nothing," I muttered through the side of my mouth, lighting the cigarette and pushed the window open.

"I'm going to pretend you're not killing your lungs right now and focus on the more pressing matter. When are you coming home?"

Taking a deep exhale, I blew it out the window. "Hopefully tonight." I let my gaze drift over the courtyard and out beyond where my freedom lay.

"Tonight?" Nikki squealed. I moved the phone away from my face with a grimace. "What do you mean tonight? I thought you didn't know where you were?"

"I don't." I tapped the ash on the windowsill. "But apparently, my jail keeper is going to be out tonight, and I've been invited to some mysterious gathering outside the barrier."

"Oooh. Your first party invite." I could hear the grin in her voice. "Are you excited? Nervous? Think you'll kiss a boy?"

My lips tugged down at the sides as my mind drifted back to the vision I had of Dex. "No. Definitely not. But I will be out of the barrier, and you'll be able to find me. So, I figured I'd message you as soon as I'm out. Then you search for me. You'll tell me where the nearest town is, and once I've made a decent enough of an appearance not to seem suspicious, I'll make a break for it. I'll hide out until you can come get me, or at least find a bus station."

"That sounds like a lot of this relies on me being able to find you on the app."

I inhaled deeply, blowing out the smoke as I said, "I have complete faith in you. If all else fails," I began but was cut off by a knock on my door. My brows furrowed, I sat my cigarette on the edge or the windowsill and walked across the room.

"If all else fails what, Elle?" Nikki probed me as I turned the doorknob.

"I'll send you a smoke signal big enough to make the news." I smiled to myself, but the moment I saw Dex's chastising face frowning down at me, my expression slid into neutral. "I'll have to call you back."

Hanging up the phone, I sat it done on the desk. "Can I help you?" I didn't know which reason Dex was here for. There were three potential reasons for his visit. Dharma? The vision? Or the mercifully given chance to escape the clock was ticking down to?

Dex lifted my bag. "You forgot this when you ran away."

I snatched my bag from him, being careful not to touch his hand. I did not want a repeat of whatever caused that vision in his class.

"Thanks. Bye." I tried to close the door on him, but he shoved in passed me. "Uh, excuse me. This is my room. Talk about privacy."

Dex ignored me heading straight for the window. "Not when you're living here." He lifted the cigarette from the windowsill and then without a word burned it to a crisp in between his fingers.

"Hey. I wasn't done with that." I huffed, chunking my bag to the side. "How'd you even know it was there? Do you have some kind of magical smoke detector or something?"

Dex leaned against my desk, his eyes flicking to the books on top. "I see you visited Sarah. That's good. You could learn a thing or two from her. And I saw you."

"Saw me?" I cocked a brow. "Like in a vi—
"

"From the courtyard." He interrupted me with a flat look, picking up the book I'd been flipping through. "If you're going to break the rules, at least pretend to hide it."

I ate up the space between us and grabbed the book from his hands, putting it back on the desk. "I wasn't given any rules. So how should I know if I break them?"

Scowling, Dex crossed his arms over his chest and shook his head. "You have to make everything difficult, don't you?"

I rolled my eyes. "Like you have any room to talk. I told you I didn't have the same powers, and you wouldn't listen. Too butt hurt over some made up wrong I've done."

"You should have told me you were a student." Dex pushed off my desk, leaving us practically chest to chest, his dark eyes boring into mine.

"And you shouldn't hit on anything with tits and a pulse," I shot back. My heart raced at our closeness. Wanting and dreading touching him again.

Dex's voice lowered until I had to strain to hear my eyes locked on his perfect lips. "Are you even going to ask about Dharma?"

I jerked back as if slapped. "I figured since no one was chasing me out that she's fine."

"Do you even care? If she'd been damaged beyond repair, would you even blink?"

I gaped at him. Then I slammed my mouth shut and, with anger billowing up in my chest, did something I never did. I touched him. On purpose.

Shoving my finger at his chest, I braced myself for the sweet caress of his lips. The hot need that filled my body before. But this time, much to my relief and horror, I felt the sharp slice of pain from a sword. Blood trickled down the side of my mouth—no, his mouth—and someone was screaming in the distance.

A warm hand latched onto my wrist, and I shoved the image away, giving him instead an easier one to swallow as he probed at my mind. The vision of Dharma's death.

He gasped, his eyes flying open as he stumbled back from me and released my wrist.

"That's what I not only see, but *feel* every day." I walked toward him, watching as he took a step back for each one I took closer. "Think about that the next time you ask me if I even care." I grabbed the door frame in a tight grip while Dex stared after me with mixed emotions. "I'd explode if I had to care anymore." To my surprise I didn't slam the door in his face. All the energy left me, and I sagged against the door until it shut with a small click.

CHAPTER

12

AYDEN KNOCKED ON my door shortly after nine. Like before, she didn't wait to be asked in. "You're going to wear that?" Her eyes skimmed my shredded jean shorts and black crop top.

"What's wrong with it?"

She placed her hands on the hips of her clinging red dress and sighed. "Your shirt has holes in it. I can see your bra!"

I glanced down at the hot pink bra peeking out the strategically placed holes and shrugged. "So? It's not my nipples. Are you even wearing bra?" I arched a brow, jerking my chin toward her headlights.

Quickly covering her chest with her arms, Ayden's face turned beet red. "Leave me alone. I can't wear one with this dress."

"Then why didn't you wear something else?" I bent down to put my boot on over the just as holey fishnet tights I wore beneath my shorts.

"It's a party."

"And?"

"And..." She trailed off, turning her face to the side as she tapped her fingertips together. "And Bishop will be there."

My brows rose. "Ohhh. Ayden likes the broody type, does she?"

"He's not broody. He's deep," Ayden countered, and stomped to the door. "Come on before we're late."

"And he's a mental on top of it." I mock clucked my tongue at her. "Oh, Ayden. What would everyone say?" We quickly and quietly hurried down the hallway.

"Shut up, you. Or I'll tell everyone you have the hots for a teacher."

I startled back, pausing in place. "No, I don't. I mean, I don't know what you're talking about."

I thanked the shadows of the hallways for hiding my expression. Dex was unbelievably hot, sure. But I needed a bit more than attraction to be into someone.

What about the vision? You obviously don't need much more if that's any indicator of your future.

I shoved my inner bitch down and focused on staying unseen or heard. I couldn't let my one chance to get past the barriers to get blown because I was distracted. Especially, not by a teacher.

Once we were out of the school and walking down a cobblestone path, I felt safe enough to ask, "Where are we going again?"

"Just wait." Ayden grinned and skipped a dance. Spinning full circle, she let her arms swing happily around her. "It's going to be like nothing you've ever seen before. I've only ever gone to one before this, and it was just..." She sighed, clasping her hands before her as she stared up at the starry sky.

"That good, huh?" I kind of felt bad about missing it. But I had to get out of here. I didn't belong. No matter how much my dad thought I did. He hadn't cared enough to save Mom, so who said he even cared now?

You know you're wrong. That irritating voice was back again. *He wouldn't have brought you here if he didn't. He could have let the angels find you.*

Conflicted by what I'd always known about my dad and what had happened recently, I couldn't bring myself to find a reason to stay. This so-called danger hadn't shown itself. Everyone just said I was in danger outside of the school, but besides my dad and Azazel, I'd yet to meet an angel. Certainly not one who wanted to kill me.

I rubbed at the mark on my hand, which had faded even more since I'd arrived. Sarah told me it would disappear completely eventually, but guessing when exactly that would happen was like guessing Nikki's favorite celebrity crush, which changed on a daily basis, if not hourly. That girl fell in love far faster than I ever thought healthy or possible.

The stars and moon lit the way until the cobblestone turned into a dirt path and the gates surrounding the school disappeared with a slight pop of air around us.

"That was strange."

Ayden gave me a knowing nod. "Going through the barrier the first time is weird for everyone. You'll get used to it."

I hummed in agreement, though I had no plans to get used to it. I clutched my purse and phone closer to my side. I'd have liked to bring more with me, but I couldn't let myself look suspicious. I barely got away with the conservative outfit I'd picked out. No way was I trying to hitch a ride or get on a bus wearing a tiny dress. That was just demanding more attention than I needed or wanted right now.

"We're almost there!" Ayden reached out to grab my hand but stopped herself. "Oops. Sorry."

I shook my head and smiled, holding my hand out. "It's fine. I won't bite."

Ayden glanced down at my hand chewing on her lower lip. "Doesn't it hurt you though?"

I shrugged. "I'm used to it."

"That's okay." She offered me a shy shrug. "I don't want to do anything that'll cause you pain. I'm just happy you're here."

Surprised by her choice, I lowered my hand. Most people jumped at the chance to ignore my discomfort. Anything for them to pretend like I was normal. Ayden's words sliced at my guilty conscious once more.

I followed after her, keeping to myself as I watched her basically dance a whole musical number down the trail into woods I hadn't known were so close to the school. Eventually, laughter and real music could be heard to go along with Ayden's dancing. The dark trees around us lit up with red and yellow light. People awed and cheered. Ayden jumped in place and glanced back at me.

She clearly wanted to run ahead, so I waved her off. "Go on. I'll catch up." My lips tugged up at the edges, unable to hold my sobering mood with the infectious grin on her face.

Not having to be told twice, Ayden took off into the woods, leaving me alone. Taking a second to check for others, I pulled my phone out and shot a text to Nikki. I didn't have to wait long for her response.

Nikki: Nevada? Why the heck would you be all the way out there?

It was worrying. My dad hadn't only taken me out of the state, but across the country. It was far from Nebraska. It would take more than one bus to get back home, and no way could Nikki get me.

I shot her a text back, letting her know I'd message her when I left.

Nikki: Be careful.

Sticking my phone in my back pocket, I hurried forward. Couldn't give Ayden a reason to come looking for me. At least not now. It was far too early.

When I broke the clearing, a full out party raged in front of me. Students hung around big bonfires and drank from red cups, laughing and playing around. Some of them were already too drunk to stand.

Nephilims weren't that different from human teenagers, it seemed.

I walked around the bonfire, being careful not to brush up against anyone. Someone held out a cup to me, and I took it without saying thank you. Not that they'd have heard me anyway. The girl who'd given me the cup had her tongue down the throat of another girl who I recognized from my Intro to Enoch class.

Humming my amusement, I sipped from my cup and meandered around the area. It took all of ten minutes for me to get cornered by Charity, Bishop, and the guy from the smoking spot.

"What are you doing here?" Charity growled, getting in my path when I tried to walk away.

"I was invited."

"Well, I'm uninviting you." Charity tried to take my cup, but I spun around in place keeping her from taking it.

I narrowed my eyes on her. "Apparently, we're back to mean girl mode, huh? No secret cigs between classes anymore? Ah, what a shame." I mock snapped my fingers before taking a drink of my cup, my eyes on her the whole time.

"That was before you basically put Dharma in a coma, you freak!" Charity screeched, putting her hands on her hips as she got into my face.

I held my hands up and out to the side. "Hey, I was just doing the assignment. It's not my fault your friend doesn't know how to take the memory she is given." I sighed and stared down into my cup. "Some memories deserve to stay buried."

Then to my utter horror, Charity burst into tears. Bishop patted her on the back awkwardly while the other guy glared at me as if I'd hit her in some way.

"All...she...wanted..." Charity hiccupped, and a whining sound came out of her nose as she cried. She patted Bishop on the arm, which was apparently code for *you tell her*, 'cause he turned that emo hair sweep in my direction.

"Dharma was just trying to protect everyone."

I frowned. "From me? How does digging in my brain protect anyone? It obviously didn't help her."

My comments only made Charity cry harder, and now it was pot guy's turn to step in.

"We've had numerous sightings of angels nearby, and she needed to make sure you weren't an angel pretending to be one of us."

Okay, so now I felt bad. Well, worse actually. Sure, Dharma had been asking for it, but I didn't mean to mess her up completely, just scare her off a bit. Still, there was something about their accusation that bothered me.

"Why did you think I was?" I cocked my head to the side. "None of the teachers do."

"Exactly," Bishop pointed out. "You didn't have a trial period. You didn't get escorted by an elder for the first six months. Not like the rest of us. Plus, you're..." His eyes went up and down my form with a conflicted expression.

"I'm what?"

"Older."

I leaned forward, afraid that I'd misheard him over the music and Charity's wailing. "What? What does my age have to do with it? Aren't you all high schoolers?" I gestured around the bonfire.

Bishop nodded. "Yeah, but every one of us save Ayden got here when we were just showing our powers, around thirteen years old. Or if their parents knew about their powers even younger. You're what, twenty?"

I sputtered in my drink. "Excuse me. I'll have you know I will be nineteen in two months. Besides, I'm hardly ancient."

"But you've had your powers longer. You should have been found before now." Bishop and pot guy stared me down, as if expecting me to sprout wings then and there.

"I don't have to explain myself to you, but because I feel bad for hurting your friend, I'll say this once and only once. I'm not, nor have I ever been, an angel. I didn't even know they existed until two days ago!"

"Elle!" An excited squeal broke through my standoff with them. "There you are. They're about to start!"

I twisted around to see Ayden, who then collapsed against me. Apparently, she was too drunk already to care that she broke her no touching rule. I flinched against her death, but then had to struggle to keep her upright.

"Geez, someone can't hold their liquor," I wheezed, trying to keep her from knocking me to the ground.

Ayden giggled and tapped my nose. "You're pretty. I bet you have had tons of sex. Unlike me. Who's a complete vir—"

"Hey!" I cut her off and turned her toward the others looking on. "Look! It's Charity and

Bishop! And..." I blanked as I tried to recall if I actually knew the pot guy's name.

"Blake," he supplied helpfully, eyeing Ayden up and down as if she were a prospective treat.

"Yeah. Well." I shifted until I had a better grip on Ayden. "It was nice chatting with you all. Let's not do this again." I gave them a stiff smile before half dragging Ayden away. Finding a bench near the bonfire, I asked, "What's this thing you wanted me to see?"

"What thing?" Ayden stared up at me blankly.

"You know, the once in a lifetime thing you told me I had to come see," I tried once more, wondering what the hell was in her drink.

"Oh yeah. The thing. It's starting, but we have to..." She tried to stand up, but her world went sideways, and I had to catch her again. "It's that way." She pointed a wagging finger toward a little pond not far off.

"Okay. Good. Let's—" I caught sight of the twins. "Hey, Zephyr and...uh fuck, Bayu. A little help here?"

The twins turned from who I now saw was Coral and Joash and rushed toward me.

"Geez, Ayden. Getting started early it seems?" Zephyr chuckled, looping his arm under her legs and lifting her up. Thankfully, her skirt was long enough not to show off all her goods to the party as we walked her over to the pond.

"So, what's this miraculous thing that's supposed to happen tonight?" I drained the last of my cup and crushed it in my hand.

We leaned Ayden up against the back of a log laying on its side on the ground before sitting on it ourselves. Coral sat next to Joash, her eyes barely leaving him for a second, and the twins sat on either side of Ayden. I sat at the end next to Zephyr, who left a good half a foot between us.

"It's kind of a show," Zephyr answered, his eyes focusing out on the pond. "All of the elementals come together and let our powers intertwine, becoming one together in a dance of sorts, but it looks like Ayden here isn't going to get to do it this year." He bumped her on the shoulder as she snorted and snored, leaning her head against his leg.

"So, kind of like how you used your wind and fire powers on that first day?" I leaned forward so I could see all of them.

"Kind of, but to a larger extent, and we have a lot more space to work with." Joash spread his arms out to measure the pond length.

Coral grinned happily and bobbed her head in agreement. "It'll be pretty cool looking. Especially to someone who hasn't seen that kind of stuff, like you."

I rocked in my seat a bit. While my nerves were buzzing to get on the road, I was a bit hyped up to see what they were all going on about. After all, it was a once in a lifetime show. I couldn't miss it, could I?

CHAPTER 13

AS IF ON an unspoken command, everyone at the party quieted. Those who were around the bonfire doused the flames and made their way over to the pond. A hush came over the water as everyone gathered around.

Something in the air, like a sort of pressure, danced across my skin, setting my hairs on end. The twins lifted their hands before them while Joash held a single hand out. Coral clasped her hands before her as if praying.

"Watch." Ayden sobered up enough to grab my ankle.

I jerked my eyes back to water, waiting for whatever was going to happen next.

Suddenly, the sky went dark. The moon and stars, which had shone down on us before, were now blocked out by the clouds. Clouds that hadn't even existed until just now.

The entire clearing was pitch black. I couldn't even see my fingers in front of my face. Then a single glow, a drop of light that was barely a blip, burned in the middle of the pond. The single drop of fire turned into two, then three, multiplying until there were so many, I couldn't count them. They grew and morphed until a faceless featureless form developed from each one of them, not more than a foot tall.

As if to some unheard music, they began to dance and spin, twirling around in skirts of flames across the water. In sharp and fast movements, their arms and legs punched out and kicked to the sides.

Each fiery figure darted about the water, causing ripples to spread out, small at first and then larger, until the entire surface undulated with micro waves. The waves shifted and curled, folding in on themselves as they gathered together into their own glowing faceless and featureless figures. They pranced around the water in fluid happy movements, much different than that of their fiery counter parts.

The fiery figures seemed annoyed by the water figures dance. They stopped in place, shaking as they watched the water figures skip and hop across the pond surface, their ripples causing the ones created by the fiery figures to mesh and collide. The fiery figures heads turned to each other and seemed to nod in agreement before they darted across the pond in a flash. The water figures didn't see them coming as they shoved past them. Their fire hissed at the contact with the water, filling the scene with steam.

The water figures paused in their dance, watching cautiously as the fiery figures spun and spun until I felt as if the world itself was moving. I clutched the wood beneath me, letting the pain of the bark bite into my hands to ground me. I'd never seen anything like the sight before me. When Ayden had told me it was once in a lifetime, I'd thought she was exaggerating. My guilt of leaving had been pushed to the side from the vision of the dance before me. I thanked whoever might be listening that I'd decided to stay for this.

"Keep watching." Ayden was sitting up now, her eyes on the dance before us. "The best part is coming."

I turned my gaze back to the pond, searching for what might happen next.

The fire and water figures were in a standoff of sorts. Each one of them doing their own form of dance, trying to outdo the other. A rumble beneath our feet startled me, but one look around the pond and I relaxed. No one else seemed bothered by it.

The fire and water figures battled it out on the open surface, unaware of the growing ripples bubbling up from the center of the pond. A darkness pushed against the surface, pulsating and fighting to the top. When it broke the top, a large glowing green figure with wings made of leaves and branches spread out the length of the pond.

The mother nature type figure loomed over the fire and water figures. They stopped their fighting, gaping up at the giant before them.

The water figures scrambled over themselves, pushing past the fire figures to get closer to the green giant. They cuddled up to it, letting themselves be absorbed into its form, allowing the green giant to grow bigger and stronger by their sacrifices.

The fire figures, though, were different.

They stared up at the giant with awe and fear, but not many went closer. Those who did venture toward the giant burned it wherever they touched. The giant swatted at them, knocking them off their feet and into the watery depths below.

When the other fire figures saw this, they grew in form and anger, charging at the giant as one. The green giant batted at them like buzzing gnats, but there were too many of them. The fire overcame the giant, burning it down until there was nothing left but burnt earth left in the middle of the watery grave of their friends.

Then one by one, the fire figures sagged and slowly walked into the water, letting it envelope them as they hissed and bubbled out of existence, leaving us in complete darkness.

Silence filled the clearing, and then a sudden thunderous applause erupted. People hooted and hollered. Someone lit the bonfire back up, and the clouds covering the sky were blown away.

I shifted to the others with a mixture of emotions in my chest. It wasn't hard to figure out what the whole performance depicted. The battle of the angels versus the fallen. The green giant was meant to be God. However, the ending was what stumped me. If the fallen found God to be the evil, then why did they seem so sad at the end of it all?

"So, what did you think?" Zephyr turned to me with a curious smile.

Shaking away my philosophical thoughts, I smiled back at him. "It was great. Really. You guys were right, it was like nothing I'd ever seen before. I'm glad I came."

"Good." Bayu beamed at me from the other side of his brother. "We are too. We don't get many mentals who are as easy going at you."

I burst out laughing.

"What?" Bayu asked, glancing to his brother and back to me. "What did I say?"

Shaking my head, I waved him off as I stood. "Nothing. Don't worry about it."

"Where are you going?" Ayden shifted against Zephyr's leg, her glassy eyes now clearer than before. "The night's still young."

I chuckled down at her enthusiasm. "Yeah, but I'm tired. I think I've had enough excitement for the night."

"So have you, for that matter." Bayu placed his hand on Ayden's head, making her swat at him for messing up her hair.

"Oh, okay, Dad. Thanks for the advice." Ayden giggled, but Bayu frowned at her.

Huh. Did Bayu like Ayden? Not surprising, the twins stayed attached to her side every time I'd seen them. Sadly, though Ayden only seemed to have eyes for Bishop. She was searching for him as we spoke.

"Well, I'm going to find another drink." Ayden wobbled to her feet, winking at me. "Do you need me to walk you back?"

Smirking at her inability to walk straight, I shook my head. "No, but it looks like you might need some assistance. Are you sure you should drink some more?"

She blew a raspberry and waved a hand at me. "I'm fine. It's more these shoes than my alcohol level. Besides, the performance always sobers me up." She played it off, but I wasn't so sure.

I shifted to the twins. "Can you keep an eye on her? Not that I don't think you would anyway, but I don't want to find out she fell in the pond in the morning."

Zephyr laughed and looped his arm around Bayu's shoulders. "Don't worry, we got this. This isn't our first Ayden rodeo."

I laughed with them, shaking my head, but my guilty conscious was eased by knowing I wasn't leaving Ayden on her own.

I didn't bother telling Coral and Joash good night, since they were too wrapped up in each other. Well, if their mouths molding together were anything to go by. Good for her.

Happy that my weird wacky trip into the Nephilim world would end on a good note, I dug my phone out of my purse and started toward the dirt path. I shot a text off to Nikki, letting her know I was leaving the party, then pulled up the map app on my phone.

Lifting it up so I could see it better, I stared at the little numbers telling me how long it would take me on foot to get to the nearest town.

"Three hours?" I gaped at it in horror. My dad had to pick somewhere that was out in the middle of nowhere. Why couldn't he have picked somewhere that was conveniently next to a bus stop or even a taxi service? On that thought, I tried to use ride pick up app, but I was too far out for anyone to come get me.

"Just my fucking luck."

I scowled and threw my purse over my head, looping it across my chest as I got ready for the long trek to town. It was a good thing I'd worn my boots. There was no way I'd have made this walk in heels.

When I got out of the woods and back onto the cobblestone path, I took one more glance at the school. I hadn't been here long enough to get attached, not that getting attached had ever been a problem for me. Still, there was something bittersweet about leaving.

I sighed and changed directions. Instead of going into the school gates, I took the path leading to the driveway and then that to the road. No one stopped me. No one was even out to care. It was all a bit anticlimactic, if I was being honest.

A part of me wanted someone to come after me. To tell me to stop and stay. That I belonged here. Not the sane part, but that small part that still thought that there was a place for me in the world. If today had shown me anything, that wasn't or would never be true. I was a freak amongst the freaks, and that was just the way it would always be.

I got about a mile or two down the road and was already fed up with the walking. My mouth had long gone dry, and I wished I'd at least packed some provisions for the walk. I'd have tried my hand at hitchhiking, but no cars came down the road. It was as if the world didn't even know the school existed. Though, there was a street leading to it as well as a sign I passed on the way out.

Fallon Academy for the Gifted.

I scoffed when I'd seen it. Really? They couldn't have been more creative? Like misspelling fallen was really going to throw anyone off.

And academy for the gifted? Yeah, right. Cursed more like.

If I was really gifted, I could make someone stop and give me a ride. Someone right now. I paused on the street and closed my eyes tightly, focusing with all my might. Come on. Come on. Come on. Some nice old couple come down and see this poor defenseless girl walking on the side of the street. And they just have to give her a ride. It's dangerous to be walking alone at night.

I peeked an eye open. Nothing. Nada. I sagged with a heavy breath. Fuck.

I didn't exactly expect it to work, but one could dream.

Kicking the ground as I walked, I grumbled to myself about everything that had gone on since Officer Rhoades had shown up on my doorstep. I almost went blind when a set of high beams blasted me in the face.

I threw my arm up to cover my eyes and stepped back as the car blew by. I spun around and flipped it off. "Fuck you too, buddy!"

To my shock and horror, the car stopped. It slowly backed up, and with each foot, I started walking again. Crap. The one time I prayed for someone to pick me up, and someone almost runs me over. Now they were coming back because they missed.

Unfortunately, the car was faster than I was, and I found myself staring into the tinted passenger window of a black sedan. I frowned and watched the window buzz as it slid down, revealing my dad's disappointed face.

Shit.

"Eleanor." My dad's voice came out neutral, but I could sense the anger he was holding back as he stared at me. "I have to say I am surprised to see you, out here, past the barrier, in the middle of the night, alone."

"I'd say it is quite a surprise to me as well."

Of course, fucking Azazel leaned over the center console and peered at me through my dad's window. Double shit.

"Well, you know. It's a nice night, and I thought a long walk would do me good. You know, clear my head after everything." I tried to play it off like it wasn't a big deal as I began to walk again.

Sadly, they didn't take that answer well. The car stopped completely, and the passenger door opened. I didn't stop walking, even when my dad's presence was right behind me.

"Eleanor."

"Elle," I corrected him again, not even bothering to look back at him as I glanced down at my phone. Not even halfway there before I got caught. Damn.

"Elle, I don't know how I can make you understand the danger of you being out here on your own. I'm not even thinking about how you even got out." He muttered something under his breath that sounded like a curse, but didn't elaborate further.

"I'm going home." I shot over my shoulder. "You have no right to keep me here."

"I have every right. I'm your father." He grabbed my shoulder and pulled me around.

I jerked back from him. "No. You might have donated your...seed." I threw a disgusted hand at him. "But you didn't raise me. Mom did. You only came around when we were convenient." I tried to stalk away, but his hand latched onto my elbow, keeping me in place no matter how much I pulled. He was stronger than he looked.

"I know I wasn't there for you, but there were extenuating circumstances. Ones that I will not go into here." His eyes grew worried as he scanned the area around us. "We are not safe, Elle. The block I put on you and your powers has almost faded. I can't put a new one on until it's completely gone. I'd prefer it to be behind the school's barrier."

I stared down at the mark on my hand and then glowered at my dad. "I don't know exactly what this does, but I know I'm not letting you do anything to me here or back at your mutant school."

"Nephilims. Not mutants." My dad rolled his gaze to the heavens before placing his face in his hands. With an exhausted breath, he lifted his head but the expression on his face wasn't that of an annoyed parent but of alarm, even fear. "Elle, get in the car."

"What?" I griped my purse to me tightly. "No. I'm not going—"

"Get in the car now." He grabbed me and shoved me behind him as Azazel opened her side of the car.

The sound of wings beating against the ground drew my attention, and I struggled to see around my dad. Of all the things I'd seen and experienced in my life, nothing prepared me for what stood before us. The menacing looking handsome man with wings expanding six feet on either side with a glowing sword in hand and golden armor coating his body wasn't anything like anyone I'd ever seen before.

It was then I realized that for the first time in my life, I was looking at an honest to God angel.

"Batariel, I should have known it would be you protecting the abomination," the man sneered at my dad, who to his credit, didn't flinch.

"Michael." My dad snorted, his hand going to the side. A curved blade appeared in his hand out of thin air. "You've fallen so far out of His grace, He's having you run errands?"

"Dad..." I went to put my hand on his shoulder, but large black wings popped out of his back, blocking me from touching him as well as seeing the angel.

"Azazel," my dad ordered from the other side of the wings. "Get her out of here."

Sharp nails bit into my arm, and I was shoved into the passenger side of the car before I knew what was happening.

"Wait." I tried to open the door, but it was locked. Glaring at Azazel, I growled, "Let me out. We can't leave him there."

Azazel didn't even spare me a glance, putting the car into gear and speeding off as something crashed and shook the ground. "Your father can handle it. My job is to keep you safe."

Twisting in my seat, I tried to see what was happening behind us, but we had gotten too far away already to make anything out. Flashings of light in the distance were the only sign that anything was going on.

"Do you have a death wish, girl?" Azazel switched gears violently as we pulled into the gates of the academy. "You'd think that someone with your abilities wouldn't put themselves in unnecessary danger."

One would think.

CHAPTER

A KNOCK ON my bedroom door woke me up from my usual dream. This time, the shadows were closing in on me, whispering, "We've found you, at last."

I didn't want to think too much into what it meant. It was too conveniently associated with my recent angel encounter to be a coincidence.

The persistent knocking continued as I rolled over and shoved my pillow over my head, trying to block it out. My dad still hadn't come back from fighting with Michael. Normally, I would attest his missing person to Bart being Bart, but under the circumstances, it could be bad. Very bad.

The knocking turned into a pounding.

"Motherfucker," I grunted, turning over and climbing—well falling—out of the bed. I tripped over my shoes and barely caught myself on the doorknob. "Who put those there?" I shot daggers at my favorite boots, shoving my hair out of my face and unlocking the door. Pulling it open with a scowl, I prepared to give whoever interrupted my sleep a piece of my mind.

"What do you…want?" My mouth fell open at Dex standing on the other side of my door.

His masculine arms were crossed over his chest, and his dark gaze was skimming over my pajamas, which consisted of a tank top and short shorts.

"Uh…what are you doing here?" I shifted slightly behind the door, hoping to hide the fact that I wasn't wearing a bra right now.

Dex stared hard at me, lingering on my bare legs.

"Hey!" I snapped, snapping my fingers in his face. "Eyes up here, buddy."

Blinking rapidly, Dex cleared his throat and turned his face to the side. "Get dressed. You're late for breakfast."

I stared at him dumbly. "So?"

"So," Dex began, pushing into my room without permission. "Your little stunt last night has consequences." He found my discarded uniform and tossed it at me without looking.

"That doesn't explain what you're doing here."

Dex grabbed my books and shoved them into a bag. "I'm your babysitter."

I pulled the skirt over my shorts, not bothering to take them off. I pushed around Dex and grabbed my bra from last night. "I'm too old for a babysitter."

Dex stared hard at the hot pink bra I was shaking at him. "Obviously, not." He shook his head and took a firm stance. "Azazel has assigned me to make sure you go to classes and actually integrate with the other students."

"Why?"

"Because maybe you'll stop trying to get yourself killed if you actually want to be here."

I snorted. "Azazel took my cell phone so it's not like I can get out, even if I wanted to." Nikki was probably going crazy when she didn't hear from me again. Not that Azazel cared about some silly human.

Dex moved to the door and waited. "Get dressed. I'm not leaving until you do. Don't make me come back in here."

"Or what?" I arched a brow, laughing at how serious he was taking this all. "You'll spank me?"

Dex's dark eyes heated, and his jaw clenched, making me feel even more naked than my skimpy pajamas already did. "Don't tempt me."

"That's not what I—" I cut myself off with a shake of my head. "Forget it." I shut the door in his face, sinking my hot face into my hands.

What the hell was I doing? Spank me? I'd never said something like that in my entire life.

I was so mortified. Why didn't Michael just come and kill me now? Save me from myself already.

A thunk from the other side of my door reminded me Dex was still waiting on me. I hurried to change out of my tank top and into my bra and school shirt. I picked up the necktie and gave it a long look. Sighing, I looped it under my collar and tied it into a bow. I grabbed my bag and pulled my boots on before heading to the door.

"Ready?" Dex lifted a brow, pushing off the door frame.

I didn't answer him. No, I wasn't ready to pretend everything was okay. I wasn't ready to act like I belonged here when I didn't. My hand tightened on my bag, and I dipped my head. I wished Mom was here. She'd know what to do.

My babysitter stayed silent for the most part as he escorted me to breakfast. The others were nursing massive hangovers, so it was a pretty quiet affair all together. None of them knew what had happened to me after I left the party, and I planned to keep it that way.

"Hey." Ayden tapped her spoon against my hand. "Why the long face? You didn't drink near as much as the rest of us. Plus, we got busted by Professor Rufus shortly after you left. Detention for the rest of the semester." She rolled her eyes but smiled. "Besides, you have the hottie Dex giving you the hungry eyes."

"What?" I made a face before turning in my seat to search out Dex at the back of the dining hall. He was indeed watching me, but I wouldn't call the look on his face hungry, more like annoyed. Which I couldn't blame him. Who wanted to play babysitter to a grown woman?

"For real." Coral gave a wistful sigh. "You're so lucky. Every girl with two brain cells to rub together has had a crush on Dex at some point or another during their stay here."

I shot a look back to Dex for a moment and then back to them. "How old *is* he?"

Ayden shrugged. "Who knows? We don't exactly age the same as humans. Could be a few decades, could be centuries. Hard to tell."

"But Sarah looks like a grandma," I pointed out with a frown.

"Well, Sarah's been around for a long time. Emphasis on the *long*." Joash chuckled and slapped hands with the twins.

Coral sat next to Bayu rather than by Joash, which made me wonder if something happened between them after I left. They'd been held together by saliva and hormones last I saw them.

I don't care, I reminded myself. *I'm only here temporarily. I can't get attached to them and their problems.*

After breakfast, my babysitter stayed close on my heels, not even pretending not to be following me. His presence gained me a lot of curious glances and glares from others. Usually of the female persuasion.

The only time Dex left me was when he dropped me off at each class. Professor Rufus gave Dex an understanding look as he dropped me off at my first class. Professor Rufus avoided my gaze as I walked past him and over to my seat. Trevor was already in his and eager as ever to talk to me.

Oh boy.

"Hey, I heard there was a party in the woods last night. Did you go? Was it awesome? I bet it was awesome." He beamed, practically bouncing in his seat.

"Uh, yeah. Awesome." I shifted in my seat, my fingers tapping on the surface of my desk. I needed a cigarette bad. I missed what Trevor said as I tried to contemplate the likelihood that my guard dog would let me sneak out to have one.

"Did they? Did they?"

"Huh?" I jerked my eyes back to the boy and cocked my head to the side. "Did they what?"

"Harmonize their powers?" Trevor asked again, exasperated by my lack of response.

I thought back to the show I'd seen. The display of violence and beauty all mixed together into one. Harmonizing, huh? Well, they have that down to an art. I'd definitely call what they did a display of harmonization.

"Yeah, they did." I picked up my pencil as Professor Rufus began to write on the board. Today we were talking about the fall and rise of Lucifer, the Morning Star. Samael. Who apparently ran a high profile business office in New York City. It made me suspicious about who exactly my dad worked for. Too many coincidences.

I tapped my pencil against the side of my desk, my leg bouncing in place. I so didn't want a history lesson right now. I needed to get my phone back and let Nikki know what happened. The last thing I needed was for her to show up here. Especially since those so-called angels actually existed and wanted me dead.

Go figure.

Professor Rufus' speech became background noise as my mind wandered.

There was so much I didn't understand about this place. Or about my dad. Even everything I knew about myself was becoming more and more of a mystery. My fingers circled the mark on my hand, which was barely there today.

Sarah told me there were more to my powers, but what? How far could my powers go? I saw visions of death, which wasn't exactly something you could expand on.

It's not like I'll suddenly sprout wings and fly.

Out of the corner of my eye, Trevor's pencil rolled off his desk. It dropped to the floor and continued until it was hidden under the person in front of him.

"You dropped your pencil."

"What, where?" Trevor lifted his book up, searching for his pencil. The pencil that was underneath the edge of his book, and when he lifted the book up, it knocked the pencil off, just like I'd seen before. I watched as it fell to the ground again and rolled under the chair in front of him.

"Hey, that's not funny." Trevor stuck his tongue out at me, getting out of his chair to retrieve his pencil.

"Uh...sorry." I dragged my hand through my hair, catching my fingers in the tangles. Great. I was seeing things and had a bad case of bed head.

CHAPTER 15

WHEN CLASS WAS over, Dex was waiting right outside the doorway.

"Don't you have your own class to teach?" I shot at him, trying to quicken my steps to lose him.

"Yes, but since someone has to keep any eye on you until your father is able to, a substitute is covering my classes."

The mention of my dad made me stop. "What about my dad? Is he okay?"

Arching a brow, Dex continued to walk past me. "I didn't think you cared one way or the other."

"Well, no," I explained, catching up to him as I darted by the other students and trying my best not to hit every single one of them. "I mean, I do, but more in a curious, did-that-angel-kill-him-last-night kind of way."

Dex snorted. "It will take far more than Michael to take out your father. Besides, they don't want to kill him. They need him."

I frowned. "Why?"

He stopped abruptly, and I barely caught myself from walking into his back. "To get to this place, of course."

"What?"

"Who do you think funds this place? Keeps it hidden from the angels?" Dex stared at me as if I'd grown a second head. "Your father is single handedly responsible for finding and keeping all of these children alive." He gestured around the hallway. "He is the reason none of the angels have stormed this place and taken us all out." His expression grew serious. "We owe a lot to him."

I hummed and shifted in place, uncomfortable with the way he was talking about my dad. "So, he neglected me all my life to protect the kids of everyone else? Great to know my childhood wasn't ruined for nothing." I huffed and stalked away, not caring if he followed me or not. He would anyway.

"You have issues, you know that?" Dex's voice came from the left far faster than I expected.

I rolled my eyes. "You think?"

"Look, my mom wasn't around either. She had me, dropped me off with my dad, and took off," Dex explained, his eyes forward as we walked. "So, I understand the whole being mad at your absentee parent, but your dad..."

He huffed a laugh. "He's doing something unheard of. He's changing the world. You have to see the bigger picture."

"Yep, I got it." I gave him a sideways look. "The many for the sake of one. If I'd been in his place, I'd probably have done the same."

Dex nodded in satisfaction at my answer.

"Unfortunately," I continued on, stopping before the door to my next class, "that doesn't make up for years of neglect and letting my mom die in a horrifying car accident, but thanks for trying." I gave him a big two-handed thumbs up and grinned obscenely from ear to ear.

I didn't give him the chance to answer before I ducked into the gymnasium.

Pfft. Changing the world. Sure, fine. My dad can play superhero to the masses, but I'd stick with what I knew. A dad who didn't care enough to save his own wife from a horrible death.

"Let's all gather around," the gym teacher called out, her shorts a bright fire truck red and clashing loudly with the dark orange polo shirt. "We're going to practice those powers of awareness today."

I took one look at the pile of silk ties and balls and turned on my heel. Nope. Not gonna happen. We played that game at my old school. No way was I letting someone I couldn't see throw a ball at my face.

I rubbed my nose in remembrance. Not gonna happen.

The teacher called out to me, but I waved a hand behind me as I walked out the door. Let them give me detention.

Thankfully, Dex wasn't waiting outside the door. Maybe he had a class to teach after all?

Either way, I wasn't going to look a gift angel in the mouth. I booked it to the nearby side door leading out into the courtyard. I dug into my bag for my cigarettes and lighter, and quickly lit up before I got caught. I wasn't about to waste these precious moments or puffs on finding the perfect spot.

I hadn't even gotten halfway through my cigarette before I heard, "You're not allowed out here."

Sighing, I didn't bother look over at Dex as I took another drag of my cigarette. "Don't you have class to teach?"

"Aren't you supposed to be in gym?" He stopped beside me, snagging my cigarette out of my hand to take a drag from it.

"Do I really look like the gym going type?" I snagged the cigarette back from him with an arched brow, taking a pointed drag of it before blowing the smoke in his direction.

To his credit, he didn't even cough, but he did take my cigarette again. "You really shouldn't smoke. You're too young."

Getting tired of this game, I placed my hands on my hips and scowled. "I'm old enough. Besides, you have room to talk." I gestured to his form. "You can't be more than twenty-five."

"Actually, one hundred and twenty-five, this year."

I frowned. "Oh, yeah. The others mentioned something about that." I shook my head, pulling my hair over one shoulder. "How is that possible?" I reached into my bag for my pack of cigarettes, shimming one out, I stuck it in my mouth and fumbled for my lighter.

"We don't age like humans. A human life is only a fourth of our life spans," Dex told me as he reached out and lit my cigarette for me.

I cocked my head at him, taking the cigarette between my fingers. "I thought you were a mind reader. How can you do that too?"

"I am, but I am also a fire element." He let a ball of fire dance around on his palm and gave me a rare lopsided smile. "On my mother's side."

"Isn't that incestuous?" I sucked in a breath of smoke, this time blowing it to the side. I wasn't a complete bitch.

"Not really." Dex shrugged. "They were created by the same person, but not of the same line." He lifted the almost finished cigarette to his lips, sucking it down before using his powers to burn it into ash. "In a way, we are all brothers and sisters in God."

I scoffed at that. "Yeah, okay."

"You don't think so?"

Humming to myself, I tried to figure out how to response. "I'd never been one for religion. Or God for that matter. If there is a God—" I stopped and barked in laughter. "I suppose that's a moot point now, huh?"

Dex arched a brow, smiling slightly.

"Anyway, God's never done much for me. One way or another." I dropped my cigarette onto the stone beneath my feet and stomped it out with my boot. "So, if I had to have an opinion on Him, I'd have to lump Him in with all the rest of my experiences with dads."

Nodding in understanding, Dex didn't try to make me change my mind. He didn't try to tell me how much God cared about me and was looking out for me. I wasn't sure if it was because he didn't think so or if he just wasn't the type. It was also quite possible he thought I just wouldn't change my mind. Which was a valid assumption.

"That time in class," he began, and I stiffened. "When I saw inside your head...not the part with us," Dex explained when he saw my face. I hoped I wasn't blushing too bad. "I saw a bit of what Dharma saw. The stuff you keep in the back of your mind."

I ducked my head. "Oh." I'd rather have talked about the sexy vision I'd had. I waited for him to tell me what a freak I was, to tell me that I was an abomination.

So, when he finally continued, I was taken back. "You have a lot of pain in your heart and in your mind."

"Yeah, I guess."

I tried to shrug it off, but he wouldn't let me. Dex turned to me, his hand reaching out almost afraid to touch me.

"It must be hard, see the future."

I blinked up at him, a part of me wanting him to touch me. "It's harder to live in it."

When he finally touched the side of my face, I tried not to flinch, but some habits are hard to break. His fingers brushed a piece of hair behind my ear.

I shuddered as I was overtaken by another vision. Instead of seeing his death this time, it was another one that left me physically panting, as if it were happening to me. A hand ghosted the skin between my thighs, molten heat building with each stroke of his fingers. An involuntary sigh escaped my lips as the feeling of a hot mouth wrapped around the tip of my breast.

So overwhelmed by the visions, my knees buckled beneath me, and Dex caught me while I gasped. Staring up at him with a mixture of wonder and embarrassment, it took me a moment to gather my wits before I scrambled from his arms.

"Elle," Dex's voice was low and husky. The bulge in the front of his pants confirmed he'd seen and been just as affected as me from the vision. "Is that my future?"

I swallowed thickly, licking my lips as I breathed out, "Yes."

"When does that happen?"

His expression was guarded, as if he couldn't or wouldn't allow me to see what he was thinking. Did he want it to happen? Was the idea completely abhorrent to him? Obviously, his body didn't think so, but that didn't mean anything. Men could get hard for practically any reason.

"Time is relative. You can't always tell where you'll end up in it." I didn't have to worry about lying when answering his question. I'd never been able to tell when something was going to happen. At least, not the way he was talking about. Unless there was a clock or a newspaper or something in the vision, I had to base it off of what I saw.

Like my mother's death.

I knew the day she would die based on the clothes she was wearing in the car accident. The necklace she wore around her neck was new. She'd just bought it the week before. In fact, I'd almost collapsed the moment I saw it around her neck the first day. She'd consoled me, reminding me that the future wasn't something I could control.

Except Sarah made me think that it was. That I would be able to change the future. If I could, if I could stop the deaths I saw, then I would never have to feel the way I did when I waited for my mother to die.

To my utter relief, the large clock chimed twelve times. It was time for lunch break.

Dex shifted away from me, back to his stiffer than a dead guy façade. "We better go."

He kept his distance from me as we made our way back inside, being extra careful not to touch me. If he had anything to say about what we'd both seen, he didn't say so. Then when he dropped me off at lunch, he didn't stay to watch, but left without saying goodbye.

Well, I'd heard of being pumped and then dumped, but this was ridiculous.

CHAPTER

THE DAYS DRAGGED by in a blur. There was still no sign of my dad, but Azazel assured me that he was fine. I still had a babysitter, but it was a rotation of other teachers and staff I'd barely said hello to in passing. Dex didn't show back up once.

In class, he pretty much acted like I didn't exist. We were given assignments, most of them things that I couldn't do. Even when they wanted me to tell the future, I couldn't do it on command. I figured the thing with Trevor had been a fluke or a weird occurrence of déjà vu.

I stopped by Sarah's once that week, looking for some kind of insight into my powers, or even just a listening ear. I could use with a friend who understood what I was going through. I still hadn't gotten my phone back, and I knew it was just a matter of time before Nikki showed up with a whole SWAT team looking for me.

"Be patient," Sarah told me as she poured me another glass of her godawful tea. "I see change in the air. Worry causes nothing but wrinkles."

I snorted. "From what I hear, we're practically immortal. So, I don't think I have to worry too much about that."

Sarah smiled gently at me. "Oh, we age. I didn't get this way from drinking too much tea." She winked at she took a sip of her cup. "Tell me what's really bothering you."

I twirled my cup around in between my hands, staring down at its cooling contents. "I just feel so stuck. I'm not progressing with my powers. I'm not really learning anything but a bunch of history about stuff I don't even care about." I sighed and laid my head down on my arms, pushing my cup away. "My dad has disappeared again, so I don't even know what happened with Michael. I'm supposed to be starting college this fall with Nikki. Instead," I banged my fist on the table making the cups rattle, "I'm stuck here with no way out and I'm going a bit—"

"Stir crazy?"

"Exactly." I sighed long and hard. "I just don't know what to do. Does anyone leave this place?"

Sarah chuckled. "Of course, they do, silly girl. Do you think we keep them trapped here forever?"

I arched a brow.

Shaking her head in disbelief, Sarah shifted around in her seat to pick up a photo album. "You younglings, I'll never understand any of your generation." She laid the photo album down on the table and flipped it open to a page. "See, we don't keep them captive. This girl became a famous actress." She pointed at a pretty dark-haired girl with big curls, who I recognized from some old black and white movies. "And this boy here, why he became a football star. Won three Super Bowls." She smiled fondly as she went through each person in the book. Some went on to do amazing things, while others went on to have normal lives.

"So, what's the point of bringing us here then? Won't the angels still be hunting them down once they leave?"

She tapped her nose and grinned mischievously. "Ah, yes, but Nephilim who have been taught to shield and protect themselves are far harder to take out than mere children who are defenseless and vulnerable."

I inclined my head. "Oh."

"Which is only one of the reasons why your father wants you here."

Frowning, I shifted back in my chair. "What's the other reasons?"

Closing the photo album, Sarah set it to the side. "I'm sure you've noticed that you're not quite like the others."

My lips twisted to one side.

"It's not your fault, dear. There's nothing wrong with you." She placed her hand a few inches from mine. "Angels were never meant to mate with humans, let alone have children. The offspring of those couplings made you...the Nephilims. Which was fine for a while. Then the Nephilims began to breed amongst themselves, making even more powerful offspring. Like your friend, Dex."

I flushed at her mentioning of him. "That's why he can read minds and make fire."

"Precisely."

"And what about me?" I stared down at my hands in wonder. "I can't do any of the things the others can. I'm not even a real seer." I frowned harder as my brows drew together tight. "My dad is an angel—fallen angel, or whatever—and my mom was a Nephilim." My gaze drifted up to hers. "What about me? No one has ever mentioned what happens to people like me."

Sarah expression softened. "That's because people like you don't exist. Not only is it forbidden but near impossible." Her smile grew as she lifted her teacup to her lips. "Not completely, obviously. After all, they made you."

"But what does that mean? Will I be able to do any of the stuff everyone else can? Make fire? Read minds?" I listed all the different abilities I could think of off to her, and she simply nodded.

"Perhaps. But we won't know until it is time."

I glanced down at the mark on my hand. The one that was almost nonexistent. My dad said he would redo it here, but I hadn't seen him to worry about that conversation just yet. I didn't know if I wanted him to redo it, and yet, I could barely handle the powers I had. Did I really want more?

Thanking Sarah, I left her rooms with a lot on my mind. It was near lunch time now, and though I wasn't quite hungry, I knew I should eat something.

When I arrived at the dining hall, it wasn't as packed as usual. Searching the room, I found a familiar head of red hair.

"Hey." Zephyr gave me one of those little guy jerks of his head as he popped a grape into his mouth. None of the others were there yet. Strange.

"Uh, hey." I slid into a seat next to him because it would be rude not to and began grabbing things off the trays lining the table. After my little session with Sarah, my stomach was a bit wobbly. I choose something light. Something that wouldn't curdle in my stomach later.

"Jell-O, huh?"

"What?" I glanced away from the red pile of wiggly gelatin. "Uh, yeah. My stomach doesn't want food today."

Nodding understandingly, Zephyr popped another grape into his mouth. "That's cool. I get like that some days too. You know what helps?" He leaned toward me conspiratorially.

I decided to play along with his game. "What?"

"Don't get involved with teachers."

I jerked back. "What?"

Zephyr smirked, his brows wagging at me. "Don't pretend like something's not going on with you two."

"There isn't." I shifted, stabbing my Jell-O with my spoon.

"Then it must have been someone else I saw getting handsy with a teacher when they were supposed to be in class a few days ago." He chuckled and shook his head, sticking his fork into the pile of potato salad before shoving it into his mouth.

"That was...nothing," I ended lamely, and then my shoulders bunched up. "What's it to you anyway?"

He shook his head once more, his face clearly laughing at me. "No reason. No reason at all. Just..." he continued, as if he hadn't just said he didn't care. "Be careful. He's different. Not like the rest of us."

My fingers curled around the handle of my spoon tightly. "Different how?"

"You know," Zephyr muttered through a mouthful of food. "He's got two Nephilim parents." He frowned with concern. "I doubt there's much human in him anywhere. Probably why the girls all fawn over him so much."

"What's so wrong with that?" My words having more of a bite than I meant for it too.

"Nothing. I just—"

"And you know what? It sounds like you're just jealous," I snapped at him before he could defend himself more. "And besides that, there are plenty who would say I'm different too." I jumped to my feet, suddenly not hungry at all. "And what do you know about it anyway?"

I turned on my heel and stalked out of the dining hall. On my way out, I practically ran into Ayden and the others

"Hey, Elle." She smiled at me and then frowned when she saw my face. "Hey guys, I'll catch up." When they were gone, she shifted closer but didn't touch me. "Uh, what's up?"

"Nothing." I shifted my face to the side and then huffed. Why was I angry? I didn't know Dex. For all I knew, Zephyr had been right. Still, I didn't like the way he talked about him. Like being different was a bad thing. If anyone was different, it would be me.

Taking a deep breath, I blew it out slowly. "Nothing, really. Someone just got on my nerves. Where were you at?"

"Oh." Ayden's face lit up, and then she held her arm up. "We were getting passes for the trip to town this weekend." She showed me the metal gold bracelet around her wrist.

"To town?" My face perked up at the news. "What town? When? Where?"

Ayden giggled. "It's a thirty-minute drive to Newbury. You just have to go get a pass from Azazel."

"What about the angels?" I pointed out, not believing for a second that Azazel would let me leave the school on my own if at all. "And the barrier."

"That's what the pass is for." Ayden held her arm up again. "It works as a temporary shield to mask us from the angels, and a locator of sorts."

"What do you mean?"

"It tells Azazel or whoever monitors them where you are at all times." She twisted the bracelet around her wrist. "If you get too far away from the approved area, it sends out a sort of electrical current as a warning. If you get too far away, the current gets stronger until it knocks you out and someone will come get you to take you back to the school."

"That doesn't sound safe." It sounded more like cruel and unusual punishment to me. Another way for my dad and Azazel to keep control of their students.

Ayden shrugged, not too worried about it. "The twins tried to take off with a group of girls at one point and got knocked flat on their asses. Serves them right for trying to ditch us, but it also serves as a way to keep us safe."

"I don't see how." I arched a brow at the bracelet. I wasn't sure I wanted one of those on my wrist now.

"Because..." Ayden leaned closer to me. "Say that an angel did find one of us and they snatched us up? It would not only knock us out but whoever was touching us too." I stared at the little piece of metal with a renewed interest. That could come in handy. "So, you see, it sucks to be monitored yeah, but it's for our own good."

I hummed but didn't answer her. Ayden and the others seemed to have all drunk the same Kool-Aid here at the Fallen Academy. Arguing with her to see the light would do nothing but make her mad and isolate me from the only allies I had.

"Well, I'm going to go to lunch." Ayden shifted her book bag from one shoulder to the other. "See you later?"

I inclined my head. "Yeah, I'm going to go see about getting a pass."

"Good idea. I can show you around town!" Her amber eyes brightened considerably. "They have a little diner there that has the best milkshakes. You are going to die. I swear."

I chuckled politely at her enthusiasm. "I'm sure. I'll let you know."

"Great. See ya."

Waving bye, I headed for Azazel's office. I needed to talk to the crazy angel woman about my dad anyway, might as well try and get a pass too. Not that I had high hopes of getting one. If I was still being babysat around the school grounds, the likelihood of her letting me actually leave the school was slim to none.

When I arrived at Azazel's office, there were raised voices coming from behind her door. I sat on the bench outside of it and waited for the voices to quiet. A moment later, the door flung open and Dex stood there.

Nostrils flaring and shoulders tight, he was just as beautiful as the day I met him.

His eyes dropped to me. "What are you doing here?"

I stood and held my bag tightly to my side. "Getting a pass for the weekend."

Dex snorted, placing a hand over his face as he shook his head. "Of course, you are. No sense of self preservation." The words were muttered more to himself than to me, but I responded anyway.

"What was that?" My jaw tightened, and I stepped closer to him.

To my surprise and annoyance, he backed up a step.

"Afraid of me now, Dex?" I arched a brow, a hint of laughter in my voice.

"Stop saying my name like that." He grunted, walking away from the door. What could I say? I was a masochist, so I followed him.

"Like what?"

Dex turned his head to the side. "Like we're friends. Like you know me."

So, he was as bothered as I was by the visions. At least I wasn't the only one suffering.

"Aren't we though?" I quickened my steps until I could jump in front of him, giving him little choice but to stop or run me over. "I think we both know we're going to be more than friends."

"Not every vision comes true." Dex glared down at me with exasperation.

"Mine do."

"Well, this one won't." Dex sidestepped me and stalked away. This time, I didn't follow him.

I didn't know what his problem with me was. I hadn't done anything to him, except make him get a boner and have babysitting duties. Still, I couldn't understand why he was so against what happened in my visions. We were both adults. There was nothing wrong with us having a physical relationship. Not that I had planned on it with anyone here. Any bumping of uglies I had planned were for college, where I could get drunk and one night stand my way through the male population. That way, I didn't have to worry about them dying on me if I got too attached.

"Eleanor." Azazel's voice jerked me out of my thoughts. "Did you need something?"

I glanced back toward the direction Dex had gone and then back to Azazel. "Uh, yeah." I hurried over to her office. She closed it behind me after I stepped in. Rounding her desk, she sat behind it and clicked at her keyboard.

When I didn't say anything for a long moment and only watched her work, she stopped what she was doing and looked up at me. "Well, out with it already."

The first thing to come out of my mouth wasn't about the weekend pass or even about my dad. "What was all that about?"

"All what?" Her voice had no inflection to it at all, nor did she give away any of what she was thinking.

I opened my mouth to ask about the argument with her and Dex, and then slammed my mouth shut. What did I care? Not like she'd tell me anyway. "Nothing. Never mind."

"Then if that's all?" She turned back to her computer, but I didn't leave. "What now?" This time, she let an annoyed sigh fall from her mouth.

"I want to see my dad."

"Oh?" Her brows shot up to her hair line. "You do? That's certainly a surprise."

"Well, so? He's my dad. I can talk to him if I want." I pressed my lips into a hard line and stepped up to her desk. "And if you hadn't confiscated my phone, I could have called him myself." I held my hand out. "I want it back."

"Why? So, you can call your little friend?" She clasped her hands in front of her on the desk. "I'm afraid that's out of the question. However, I can arrange a meeting with your father, but I'm afraid he's in meetings all day today. Perhaps, Monday? Would that work for you?" I ground my teeth together. "Fine."

"Was that all?" She swiveled her chair, hopeful to have me gone.

"No. It's not." I straightened and crossed my arms over my chest, doing my best to look down on her the same way she did to me every day. "I want a weekend pass."

Her lip twitched. "Are you asking or telling?"

Seeing that I was acting like a child, I dropped my arms and took a breath. "I mean, can I please have a pass for the weekend? I'm going to go crazy if I don't get out of here. I already have someone on my butt twenty-four seven." Well, except for the fact that I'd ducked out of lunch to come here without telling my escort. "I won't even really be having free reign, seeing as those trackers you have on the students are as good as shock collars."

"I see someone told you about those." Azazel's lips curled up menacingly. "It's one of my better ideas."

"It's barbaric."

"And yet, you want one." She held her hands out to either side.

Fuck, but I did. I didn't care if it told them where I was all the time or shock the shit out of me, I needed out of this place, and now. Even if just for a little while.

"Yes..." I struggled to get the next word out, "Please."

"Very well." She reached into her drawer and pulled out a bracelet identical to Ayden's. She gestured for me to hold my arm out. Reluctantly, I did so, watching as she clasped it on my wrist. "This cannot be taken off by anyone but me. So, don't be getting any ideas." She gave me a pointed look.

"Of course not, mistress." I gave her a mock bow, the sarcasm heavy in my tone. "I live only to please you."

She snorted. "If only that were true, both of our lives would be so much easier."

CHAPTER 17

THAT NIGHT, I had the theater dream again, but this time I wasn't alone. Someone else was sitting in the theater with me. Except I couldn't tell who they were. The closer I got to them, the more indistinguishable their features became.

The projector playing the reel of my life clicked loudly in my mind, signaling the end of the film, and yet, the dream didn't end.

The shadows played in the corners watching and waiting. Not taunting me as usual.

Then for the first time ever, the projector started again. This time, the screen showed scenes I'd never seen before. Ones that weren't from my life at least. Or maybe they were ones that had not yet happened?

A blond winged man with a gleaming sword fought with a dark-haired figure on the ground. I couldn't see either of their faces, but they were both heavily beaten already. Fire burst from the dark-haired man's hand and the blond spun away from it, using his wings to extinguish the flame.

"Stop this!" I yelled, but it wasn't me, it was the me on the screen. I ran in between the two of them, throwing my arms up to block them. "This isn't going to solve anything. We have to work together."

I tried to tell myself to get out of the way, that I'd only get hurt, but neither man came after me. In fact, the moment they saw me, they were hesitant to attack. Then out of nowhere, the ground beneath our feet shook and broke. The last thing I heard before the screen went black was someone screaming my name.

I woke up in a sheen of sweat. It was still dark out, and one glance at my alarm clock said it was just after five in the morning. Too wired to sleep, I rolled out of bed and grabbed my toiletry bag. Since we were going into town today, I could put on street clothes and not wear my uniform for once. I hated that thing, and would happily burn it the moment I got to leave this place.

The hallway was quiet on my way out of my room and into the coed bathroom across the hall. I slipped into one of the stalls and sat my belongings on the provided shelf. Turning on the shower, I turned it up as hot as it would go, hoping it would wash away some of the chill my dream had left behind.

I didn't know how long I stood there in the shower, but the water tank at the school must've been phenomenal, because the hot water never ran out.

It was while I was in the middle of lathering up my hair that the door to the bathroom opened. A familiar voice called out.

"Anyone in here?"

I froze. What was Dex doing in the student bathroom?

I almost didn't answer him, but realized he could hear the water running. "Uh, yeah. I am."

There was a pause. Then heavy steps crossed the room. I could feel his presence on the other side of the shower stall door. "Is it alright if I shower here? The faculty one has been on the fritz."

More focused on the fact that I was naked in the same room as Dex than his actual words, I fumbled out, "Sure. Why not?"

It was after the shower stall next to me turned on that I realized not only was I naked, but now Dex was, and he was mere feet away from me. My eyes bore into the metal wall separating us, as if I could see through it to Dex on the other side. He must have been doing the same thing, because he didn't move around for a long moment. Then, as if a spell broke, he shifted out of the water spray, and the distinct sound of him squirting a bottle filled the room.

I washed myself at a glacial pace, wanting for some reason to prolong the time I was in there with him, even if I couldn't see him. Another part of me wanted to just hurry up and run away before I could make this any more awkward. He'd flat out refused to admit anything was going to happen between us, and yet, we were somehow drawn to each other.

Was it fate? Or maybe God was finally paying attention to me and this was how he was getting his jollies off?

"Did you get a pass for today?"

Dex's voice startled me, and I dropped my conditioner bottle on my foot. "Shit."

"Are you okay?" Dex paused on his side, and I rushed to answer.

"I'm fine. Just dropped my conditioner."

"Oh. Okay." Was that disappointment I heard in his voice?

No. I was just projecting too much. There was no way that Dex actually wanted to rush to my rescue, and yet, the dream came back to me. I didn't know why, but I had a feeling that the man fighting in my dream had been Dex, and he'd been fighting...for me.

A tense silence filled the bathroom, each of us washing on our own side. It was then that I realized I hadn't answered his question. "Azazel is letting me go today."

"That's surprising."

I snorted. "Yeah. Except, I have this nifty shock collar keeping me from getting out of line, so that should be fun." I fingered the metal bracelet. Should these be gotten wet? Since I hadn't gotten shocked yet, I figured it was fine.

"Yeah, she's quite proud of those. I remember the day she set them up. The students almost rioted." He chuckled to himself, and I couldn't help but close my eyes and savor the sound of it. Of course, that only made me imagine what he was doing over there. The water trickling down his bare skin. His muscles contracting and releasing as he rubbed over each pectoral and then down his rippling abs, taking his precious time as he made his way down his happy trail and wrapped his hand around his—

"Elle?" ·

I jerked out of my daydream so hard that my foot slipped, and I crashed to the ground. "Fuck," I groaned, rubbing my back and side where I hit the nearby bench. Much to my horror, the shower stall flew open, revealing a very naked and extremely wet Dex.

My mouth gaped open, the pain in my back momentarily forgotten as my eyes raked over him. They trailed over every inch of his deliciousness and landed on the long hard length settled between his legs.

A sharp inhaled breath from him reminded me that I was naked too. I scrambled to my feet, grabbing my towel off the hook on my way up as Dex turned his back on me, giving me a glorious view of his backside.

"Are you okay?" Dex asked, his shoulders tight and the cheeks of his ass flexed.

I securely wrapped the towel around myself and turned off the water. "Yeah, I'm fine. A bit bruised, but I'll live."

Dex jerked his head down once and then hurried back to his stall. The door closed with a clack, and the knobs of the shower squeaked as he changed the temperature.

My face heated as I imagined the cold shower he must be having now. "Dex..." I stepped to the wall separating us, placing my hand against the cool surface.

"Go get ready to leave, Elle," Dex gruffly responded, dismissing me.

Sighing, I gathered my things and walked back to my room, not bothering to change first. It was still early, so no one was in the hallway, not that I'd have cared one way or the other. When I arrived in my room, I shut and locked the door before throwing my towel clad self onto my bed.

This was bad. This was so unbelievably bad. I had the hots for Dex. Well, of course, I did. He was irrefutably handsome and sexy in a dark, dangerous way. I snorted. Dex, dangerous? He was a teacher, for one, and more angel than human. He wasn't any more dangerous than Sarah was.

Still...man, did my imagination not do him justice. I sighed longingly before forcing myself to get out of bed and get ready.

I decided on a pair of Rockstar jeans that were ripped at the knees and up the thighs, and a white ribbed tank top over a black bra. I topped it off with my jean jacket that my mom and I had bedazzled one lazy summer day. Wearing it made me feel close to her, and I needed that right now.

Once I was ready, I made my way downstairs. I grabbed a piece of toast and an apple from the breakfast table and ate on my way out the door. There was already a group of students waiting at the front for our ride.

Ayden waved at me from her group of friends. "Elle, over here!"

I meandered over to them. Nodding and greeting them each until I reached Zephyr. He offered me a small smile and nod. "Hey."

I smiled back. "Hey. Sorry about—"

"Don't worry about it." He scrubbed the back of his head and laughed. "I let my mouth run away with me sometimes."

"I gotcha. It's cool. I was having a day." The others were watching our exchange with curious glances, but didn't ask us to elaborate.

"I see you got them to let you off your leash finally," Joash commented as he shifted closer to Coral. I arched a brow. Back on again it seemed?

"Uh, yeah." I chuckled and lifted my wrist, showing off the bracelet. "Only to get a more permanent one I can't duck out on."

"What did you do to get a babysitter?" Bayu asked as we began to pile into the bus that had just arrived.

I struggled with how much to tell them. Then figured the truth wouldn't hurt. "Tried to run away while you were all getting drunk."

"What?" Ayden gasped at me as she slid into the first available seat. "Why didn't you tell me?"

I shrugged and took the seat beside her. "'Cause I didn't want you to get in trouble too."

"But why would you want to leave?" Bayu leaned over the back of our seat, astonishment in his voice. "You're safe here."

Zephyr smacked his brother on the shoulder. "Not everyone came here willingly, fucktard."

"I know that, but you didn't have to hit me, dipshit." Bayu smacked his brother back, and the two of them began to make more and more creative names for each other.

I found myself smiling as they argued back and forth. It made me wish for a sibling. Nikki was the closest thing I had to a sister. I frowned and shifted in my seat, letting the rumbling of the bus fill me.

"I would have helped you if you really wanted to leave," Ayden murmured a few moments later.

I angled my head her way. "Don't worry about it. I'm working it out."

"I knew you didn't come here on your own," she continued, her head dipped down a little bit. "And I hoped that making friends and even going to the party might help, but it seems you are determined to leave."

"It's not that." I sighed and lifted a foot onto the bench of the seat. "I just got pulled out of my life so abruptly that I didn't get to explain to anyone or even prepare. My dad..." I blew out a harsh breath. "We don't exactly have the best relationship, and he just showed up out of nowhere, dropping this bombshell on me and then disappearing. I just want answers, and no one seems to want to give them to me."

"That sucks, but I want you to know I'm here if you need to talk." Ayden reached out to touch my hand but then stopped, dropping it back down into her lap.

Smiling softly, I grabbed her hand and squeezed it tight, forcing back the flinch that came with her death. "Thank you."

CHAPTER 18

THE BUS CAME to a stop right outside of Newbury. We all piled off, and most of the students rushed off to different parts of town before their feet barely touched the ground. I loitered by the bus until Ayden and the rest of them got off.

"So, where to?" I tucked my hands into the front pockets of my jacket and waited for Ayden to lead the way.

"We're going to the game store," Bayu announced before he and his brother took off down the street.

Coral and Joash were holding hands now and whispering to each other. Coral blushed at something Joash said before murmuring, "We're going to go check out..." She seemed to struggle with an answer before Joash just led her away. She waved and flushed prettily. "Bye!"

"How much you want to bet they don't make it to a single store?" Ayden shook her head and giggled. "I swear, those two are worse than rabbits."

I watched them leave with a perturbed feeling. "They seem a bit..."

"On again, off again? Yep." Ayden popped her p's and sighed, shrugging. "They're better than a soap opera, I'm telling you."

We strolled down the road heading into town. Newbury wasn't a large town by any standards. I was used to growing up in Omaha, so this kind of place really wouldn't have done anything for me under normal circumstances. Except two weeks stuck in the Fallen Academy had me excited just to go to a diner! A diner! Somewhere I wouldn't have bothered to eat at before this all happened. Now, it was the highlight of my month.

What being quarantined will do you to you...

"It's a bit early to eat lunch..." Ayden checked her phone, and my palm itched to have my own device back in my hands. "We can walk around and check out the stores if you want? Or just find a spot and people watch?" She looked at me expectantly.

"I don't mind either wa—" I began to tell her, and then caught sight of an electronics store. "Actually, why don't we go in there?"

Ayden's mouth twisted to one side, but thankfully, she didn't argue.

I had to keep myself from running to the store so Ayden and the loitering teachers wouldn't suspect anything was up. When we walked in the electronics store, I pretended to look around, but I could already see the display for pay as you go phones.

If Azazel and my dad thought they could keep me down by taking my phone, they had another thing coming.

I just needed to get my hands on one of them, and then I could get a hold of Nikki.

While I didn't have plans right now to take off, especially after the talk I had with Ayden, I still needed to let her know I was okay.

Standing in front of the phone display was like standing in front of the holy grail. I swear, it was that monumental. I felt a huge weight fall from my shoulders as my hand wrapped around one of the plastic cases.

Until my world came tumbling down around me.

A shadow fell over where I stood, and I barely had the phone in my hands before it was plucked away by Professor Rufus with a smug grin.

"Hey, give that back. I'm going to buy that." My fingers curled into fists, and the need to knock the smirking asshole on his butt was almost too hard to refuse.

"You are on restriction." Rufus stared down at me hard, though he still had a gleeful gleam in his eyes. "That means no cell phone. You're lucky our liege even let you out of the school. I wouldn't have let you if I were running the academy." He sniffed and shifted away, pointing a finger at the door.

Clearly, someone thought they were better suited for Azazel's job, but either way, he had just ended up on my shit list. Holding back the need for violence, a valiant effort on my part if I did say so, I marched out of the store and waited by a nearby tree for Ayden to come out.

She did a few minutes later, confused and searching for me. Ayden spotted me a few seconds later and walked over to me.

"Hey, what happened? I thought you needed something."

I shook my head and kicked the stone sidewalk beneath my foot. "Nah, they didn't have what I wanted. Let's go check something else out."

As we walked, I noticed quite a bit of teachers and other staff members in town. None of them had been on the bus, I'd been sure of it.

"Do they usually come to town with the students?" I pointed out to Ayden.

She shrugged. "Sometimes, but usually it's only a few. They must be taking extra precautions this time with all the angel sightings lately." She stopped before a clothing store window and surveyed the outfit on display. "They usually just make sure that we don't use our powers or cause a fuss."

"And what about the people who live here?" I noticed a few guys about our age staring at us unabashedly. "Do they know...what we are?"

Ayden scoffed and straightened. "Of course not. They put up with us because we bring money to their little town."

"How could they not though?" I stared right back at the guys until they finally stopped and walked away. "We don't age the same, so they are bound to notice eventually."

"I'm sure they have, but none of them have said anything, or if they have, I'm sure our liege had one of the mentals do a memory alteration."

"They can do that?" My brows rose as we walked to the next store. This one had a guy making custom wood furniture. They were exquisite, if a little out of my price range. Not that I had anywhere to put it now. Until I got out of Fallen Academy, my mom's house was just going to sit there.

"Anyway, the teachers like Dex tend to stay away from town. He has too much angel blood in his system, so he ages even slower than the rest of us." She stopped at an ice cream stand and got a cone from the starry-eyed boy who wouldn't stop staring at us. "You want any?"

I shook my head no. "Really?" I asked, when we were far enough away from the boy. "He told me he was a hundred and twenty-five."

"And he barely looks over twenty, right?" She giggled, licking her ice cream cone.

It was then that I noticed we were getting a lot of looks from the town's people. "Uh, Ayden. Is it just me, or are they staring an awful lot?"

Ayden shrugged. "Humans always do that. They're drawn to us cause of our—"

"Angel blood. Yeah. I get it."

Except I didn't. No one had ever been drawn to me. If anything, they ran in the opposite direction any time I came around. Out of habit, I ran my finger over the mark on my hand, which was now completely gone. Had the mark my dad put on me also kept humans from seeing the angelic part of me as well? It was another thing I'd have to ask him when I saw him next.

Ayden stopped before an anti-aging cream advertisement. "Isn't it great that we'll never need that kind of crap?"

"Not really." I shrugged and turned away from it to keep walking.

Speed walking to catch up with me, Ayden asked, "Why not?"

"Too much time." I'd had enough of this life as it was, I had no desire to extend it even further by living practically forever.

Giving an exasperated sigh, Ayden poked me on the shoulder. "You're so bloody depressing all the time. Lighten up."

I smirked at her. "Maybe you just need to grow up."

She licked her ice cream in an obscene manner. "Nah, plenty of time for that later."

Shaking my head at her action, I grabbed her arm. "Come on, show me where this dinner is. I'm hungry."

The diner Ayden wanted us to go to was a cute little mom and pop's place. Fully made to look like a wood cabin, it was decorated from top to bottom in antlers. I tried to repress my grimace as a sweet old man seated us.

My eyes trailed over a blond guy who was far too attractive for this little town. He saw me looking and smiled. I found myself blushing as I smiled back.

I pushed the guy out of my mind, which was hard since he was right in my line of sight as we sat at our table. Once more, I was assaulted by deer everywhere. Even the table was decorated with them.

"What?" Ayden asked, grabbing her menu from the table.

Wrinkling my nose, I leaned forward a bit. "I'm from the Midwest, and even I think this is a lot of antlers."

Ayden laughed. "Don't worry, their food is way better than their decorating skills."

I hoped so.

Pulling my menu from the table, I scanned the contents. It was your basic variety diner. Cheeseburgers, fries, milkshakes, and even a few breakfast items you could order any time of the day.

"I know what I'm getting. How about you?"

Before I could answer Ayden's question, Dharma appeared at our table. I was relieved to see that she was alright, but apparently, she wasn't that happy to see me.

"What. Are. You. Doing. Here?" she practically spat in my face. She hadn't even come over with her friends, choosing to face me alone. Ballsy, but stupid.

"I'm getting lunch, duh?" I held my menu up to show her, causing Ayden to giggle.

Dharma was not so amused. "Why haven't they kicked you out already?"

I sighed. "That's what I keep asking myself, and yet, here I am. It's fabulous, isn't it?"

"No. It's not." Dharma slapped her hand on my menu, forcing it down to the table. "You are an abomination. You're not wanted here, or at our school."

"That's not true," Ayden said, trying to stand up for me. "I want her here, and so do a bunch of others."

Dharma scoffed, not noticing that we had drawn the attention of some of the diners. "Like it matters what you and your little element—"

"Club," I finished for her with a glare. "Elemental club. Right, Ayden?"

Ayden didn't catch what I meant at first, and then she noticed the blond guy from earlier. "Oh, yeah, right. Element club. We are all about studying those elements." She did a fake air punch that I would have done with a little more enthusiasm, but if the guy noticed anything strange, he didn't mention it.

"Everything okay here?" He gave a dimple filled smile that made Dharma gape and stumble over her words.

"Uh, um, yeah. We're good. Right?" She turned back to me and gave me the fakest grin she could muster.

I gave her two thumbs up and matched her smile until she giggled and left. Dharma walked backward as she smiled and giggled, waving a little bit before sitting down at her own table with Bishop and Charity.

"Are you sure you're okay?" the guy asked, tucking his hand into the pockets of his jeans. God sure pulled out all the stops with this one. He had golden blond hair that curled at the edges of his shoulders, the deepest blue eyes I'd ever seen outside of cartoons, and an ass that wore his jeans like they were made for him. To top it all off, those dimples were killer on the panties.

"I'm fine. Just school drama." I waved a hand in the air and smiled, trying to make him see we were fine.

"Oh, alright. If you're sure."

"We're sure," I answered quickly, but Ayden jumped in.

"Do you want to join us? You did save us from having to listen to her harp more. It's the least we could do."

The guy gave me a look before taking the empty seat next to me. I shoved myself so close to the wall that I was almost part of the decor. It was weird, I knew it, and he noticed.

"I don't bite, I promise." He offered me a lopsided grin.

Ayden leaned on her fist and fluttered her lashes at him. "Isn't this the part where you say only if you want me to?"

He chuckled.

Damn it.

Even that was attractive.

"I'm Ayden." She held out her hand with a flirty smile. "That's Elle. And what's your name, handsome? I don't think I've seen you around here before."

Taking her hand, Ayden practically melted into the floor as he shook it and said, "Cass. It's nice to meet you."

"Likewise," Ayden breathed out, and I had to suppress the urge to roll my eyes.

"Are you ready to order?" The sweet old man stood at our table, a note pad in hand.

Cass and Ayden told him theirs while I took a quick look at the menu and told him the first thing I saw.

"Liver and onions huh?" Cass quirked a brow. "I would not have taken you for that kind of gal."

"Well, you don't know me well enough to know what kind of gal I am or otherwise, do you?" I shot back at him, which only made him smile wider.

Holy fucking hell, was I flirting with him? This guy I just met? What the hell was wrong with me? Did this whole angel attraction thing work both ways? Except, I wasn't drawn to any of the other guys in town.

"Are you from that private school? Up the hill?"

Ayden nodded fiercely. "Yep, it's really great. We love it there." She kicked my leg under the table. "Don't we?"

I cleared my throat. "Yeah, sure. It's great." I plastered on a forced smile.

Cass didn't seem convinced. "So, are you a bunch of rich kids, or what?"

"Or what?" I answered cheekily.

Ayden choked on her water, and I handed her a napkin.

Not bothered by my answer, Cass continued, "I tried to apply there once, but they told me I didn't have the kind of parentage they were looking for." He glanced at us, as if we were supposed to fill in the blanks for him.

I shrugged. "Just a bunch of old men thinking their lineage is the best is all."

Ayden fluttered her lashes at him, "I'd let you in. In a heartbeat."

"Aren't you a cute little thing?" Cass gave her a panty melting smile that had Ayden almost combusting on the spot.

"Hmph," I snorted, and crossed my arms, throwing my feet up on the chair opposite of mine. "It's a bit too much like an occult to me."

"My professor back at the university would have loved to hear why you think so."

Cass paused as a server came by and handed out our food.

"Oh!" Ayden's voice raised a pitch. "What university?"

"Purdue in Indiana," Cass explained, picking up his cheeseburger. "I'm a history major there."

"What are you doing here?" Ayden prodded further.

"Visiting my grams," he said between bites, "but my nutty professor back at university actually believes in all the stuff they make us study. Aliens, witchcraft, and angels." He snorted and took a bite of his burger. After he chewed and swallowed, he added, "Like any of that stuff they spout can't be explained by science?"

I played with my food, not planning on actually eating any of it. "Science, right." I exchanged a look with Ayden. We really shouldn't be talking about this with a stranger.

He wiped his mouth and chuckled. "My grams swears that the teachers there don't age." Cass grinned from ear to ear. "Can you believe that load of crap?"

I didn't answer him, but Ayden laughed nervously. "Yeah, crazy."

A sudden outburst of laughter from Dharma's table had me turning in my seat. Dharma glanced in our direction and then whispered something to the table, causing them all to break out in laughter once more.

A hand shook me. My gaze went cloudy, and it was like I was outside of my body looking in as Dharma got up from her seat with a chocolate shake in her hands. She walked by our table and purposely dumped it all over Cass's lap.

"Oh, I'm so sorry," she chittered as she tried to help clean him up.

"Hey." The hand on my shoulder shook me slightly "Are you okay? There's something wrong with your eyes."

I shook my head, and my vision cleared long enough to see Dharma heading this way, chocolate shake in hand. When she got to our table, I threw myself over Cass and shouted, "Look out!"

Freezing cold liquid goop slid down my hair and into the back of my shirt. I squealed at the temperature and jumped back into my seat. Dharma and her friends laughed as Cass and Ayden tried to help me clean off.

"That's a good look for you, freak," Dharma chortled and jeered.

The bell of the diner chimed, and an authoritative voice called out, "That's enough. Everybody back to the school." Dex stood in the doorway.

Great. Just what I needed.

Cass tried to wipe my face off with a napkin, but I took it from his hand and nudged him to let me out. "Thanks, I got it."

"Are you alright?" He tried to follow me out of the diner, but I stopped before the door.

"Yeah. I'm fine. Just want to get changed."

Ayden followed the others out of the diner after paying for our meal and getting a to-go box. She hovered outside the door, waiting for me to finish wiping off.

"Are you sure you're okay?" Cass continued, staring hard at me, like those back at school used to when they realized I was different. "'Cause before, I swear your eyes, they were..."

I felt Dex's presence behind me before he spoke. "She said she was fine. Let's go."

Giving Cass a weak smile, I waved. "It was nice meeting you."

CHAPTER

DEX LEAD ME away from the diner. All the other students were being ushered back toward the bus. Dharma had apparently gotten to them, because they were all giving me dirty looks.

Wonderful. Now everyone hated me.

"She's only going to the academy because her dad runs it," one student hissed to another one, not even bothering to keep their voice low.

"I heard her mom was a Nephilim."

"No? And her dad is Batariel?" The first voice gasped in horror and disgust. "No wonder she's such a freak."

My fingers curled tightly into fists, and I hurried my steps.

Dex stayed close to my side as we left the town and arrived at the bus that would take us back to the academy. I shifted to join everyone else that was piling into the bus, but Dex grabbed my elbow.

"This way."

A flash of a vision pushed at me, leaving me breathless, but Dex did not look as if he'd been affected by this vision at all.

"Not trespassing in my mind anymore?" I followed him to a silver sports car. I wasn't about to question why I didn't have to ride with the others. Nothing in the world would make me want to do that.

Dex gave me a look. "It's safer that way." He slid into his car and waited for me to get into the passenger seat before turning his car on.

He shifted gears and pulled away from curb.

Not able to handle the tension in the car, I picked a relatively neutral topic. "I thought you didn't come to town. Too many people remembering your face?"

Dex snorted. "A simple suggestion slipped into their minds ends those theories easily."

I hummed.

"Hold on." Dex shifted gears, and the car zoomed forward, ending any conversation we could have had with his speed.

I grinned and laughed as we zigged and zagged down the road, speeding past cars and trees in a blur. If a police officer had caught our speed, he wouldn't have stood a chance at catching us. In fact, a part of me worried that Dex might crash at any moment. The braver half of me didn't care and just wanted to go faster and faster.

A sideways glance at Dex showed he too enjoyed the speed. His lips were curled up in a carefree smile, his face relaxed, and his fingers tight on the steering wheel.

We beat the bus by a landslide, pulling into the driveway of the academy. I hardly wanted to get out of the car as Dex brought the car to a stop. Except, staying there in the car with Dex was torture. All I could think about was the vision I'd just had and what I'd seen this morning. The combination of a naked Dex and the feel of his hot body pressing down onto mine was almost too much for me to bare.

Unable to handle it anymore, I opened the door and stepped out. The academy stood quiet before us as we walked up the stairs of the front building. I touched the back of my hair and grimaced when it came back sticky and brown. I gave Dex an apologetic smile. "Sorry about your car."

Dex skimmed over my ruined attire. "Don't worry about it. It's just a car. You should probably go get cleaned up." Neither one of us needed to add "before the bus gets back." I didn't want to face down any of them right now, and the ice cream was starting to itch.

I started toward my room, but Dex called my name.

"When you're done, we need to talk." His gaze was sad, as if he didn't really want to talk to me but had to.

I inclined my head, swallowing hard. "Okay. I'll be quick."

I wasn't sure what Dex wanted to talk about, but it couldn't be anything good. Was it about this morning? Nothing happened. Hell, we hadn't even kissed. Not in real life anyway. We'd done a whole hell of a lot more than kiss in my visions.

Still, I hurried to my room and gathered a new set of clothes along with my toiletries. I washed myself faster than I had in my life, even with washing my hair three times. When I was done, I quickly dried off and got dressed.

Dex was waiting for me in the hallway when I exited the bathroom. I was still drying my hair with a towel, but didn't miss the way his eyes skimmed over my newly changed clothes. By the heat in his gaze, I knew he was thinking about this morning. Unfortunately, as quickly as the look came, it was gone.

"Give me a second." I ducked into my room and put my things away, tossing my ruined clothes into the hamper. Hopefully they were salvageable. I really liked those jeans.

Cleaned and ready, I left my room and walked over to Dex. Not sure what the tone of this conversation would be, I cautiously stepped up to him. "What did you want to talk about?"

Dex began to speak, but stopped and glanced down the hallway where the sound of students returning filled the hallway. "Not here." He pivoted on his heel, expecting me to just follow after him.

Normally, I'd have been annoyed, but I wanted to know what he had to say and that required me to follow him. Regardless if I liked it or not.

Dex led me down the hallway and down past the gymnasium to a set of double doors. I knew the doors led to the library, but I had yet to need to use it just yet. Reading wasn't particularly high on the priority list right now.

Pushing the doors open, Dex gestured for me to go inside.

Becoming even more curious to know what this was all about, I only briefly oh'd and awe'd over the massive library. Any school who values education over having a new snack machine was okay in my books.

Walking over to a table, Dex placed his hand on the stack of books sitting on top.

"I'm sure you heard me yesterday in Azazel's office."

I shrugged sheepishly. "Just yelling. Nothing really distinctive."

Dex ducked his head and raked a hand through his hair. "Well, that's lucky. I wasn't exactly being respectful."

I shrugged and wandered over to the table. "I'm sure whatever you were yelling at Azazel about was well deserved. I've yelled a time or two at her myself."

Chuckling, Dex tapped his finger on the book beneath his hand. "That I can believe." He huffed and dragged a hand over his face. He was struggling to tell me whatever it was he needed to tell me.

"Just tell me." I sat down at the table and glanced at the spines of the books. *Prophecy of Zaphkiel. The End of Days. Of Fire and Ice.* And several others that were in Latin. It seemed our conversation wasn't to see about making my visions come true.

"There are things you haven't been told," Dex began, pacing before me rather than sitting at the table with me. "Things that should have been explained to you as soon as you got here. But they're so damn stubborn." He growled and jerked his hands in the air. "Everything has to be done in order and by the book. They don't realize that they're messing with people's lives. They're fallen angels, for Lucifer's sake! Breaking the rules is kind of their MO."

I frowned as I watched Dex rant and rave. I didn't know if I liked him this way. Though, I did agree that all these rules for a group of angels who rebelled against God was pretty silly.

"Dex." I half stood and reached for him. "What is it?"

Stepping out of my reach, Dex stalked over to the table. "You weren't an accident, Elle." He threw open one of the books and showed me the passage on the so-called savior or destroyer Ayden had told me about on day one.

"What about it?" I asked confused.

"Elle, your dad didn't fall in love with your mom. He picked her specifically based on a vision Sarah had." My mouth dropped open as he continued to shatter my existence into a million pieces. "He knew he could get her pregnant, and that's why he picked her. He was ordered by Lucifer to make you. A

Nephilim who was more angel than human. One who had less limits on their powers. One who could turn the tide of this ongoing battle between Heaven and Hell—Nabi. Or more commonly known as the Watcher."

Nabi!

That word. I know it. It was so familiar and yet foreign. The same name the shadows called to me in my dreams. But, why? Why would the shadows call me the Watcher?

A vague remembrance of the painting Ayden had shown me flashed in my head. The picture of the figure standing between two sides of a battle. She'd called it the Watcher as well.

It couldn't be a coincidence.

But it didn't make sense. The Watcher? Me? No way.

I shook my head in disbelief, pushing away from the table and waving my hands by my head. "You're wrong. It can't be me." I gave a bitter laugh and turned back to him. "I can't even have visions like a normal seer. All I see is death and destruction."

"And in their wake, destruction and death shall fall around them like rain. That will be the bringer of light. The savior who will cleanse the world or destroy it." Dex tapped the book with his finger once more. "It's all here, Elle. You aren't here because the angels want to kill you like the rest of us." He took a step toward me, pain in his expression as he explained. "You're here so that Lucifer can make sure that you are on our side when everything goes down. Your dad, Azazel, they didn't want you to know. They wanted you to figure out your powers on your own." He took my hands in his, but this time, I was too numb by the realization of what he said to even react to the vision. "The mark your dad put on you was to hide you from the angels as well as keep your powers in check until they were ready."

I stared down at my hand where his thumb traced where the mark had been. It had all been a lie. From the very beginning, he hadn't loved her. He hadn't even tried to save her. He only came around to make sure that his precious weapon was where it was supposed to be.

My chest heaved rapidly as I drew in short breaths of air. Something inside of me built. It roared and raged, and I feared if it didn't come out, I'd burn up from the insides.

"Let me go." I pulled my hands away from Dex, but he held on tight, locking eyes with me. "I need to...I don't know what's—"

Understanding crossed Dex's face, and he pulled me close. "Let it go. You can't hurt me."

I didn't understand what he meant, but I held on to him tight, my eyes squeezed closed as the ball inside of me wound tighter and tighter, until finally, it broke.

Wind licked at my skin, and the scent of burnt wood filled my nose. A weight on my chest had lifted, and with it, I pulled away from Dex, opening my eyes. Gasping, I jumped back.

Flames flickered all around us, but they weren't hot, and they didn't even burn. For a moment, I thought the flames had come from Dex, but then I knew. I knew it had been me.

I'd done this. The fire stayed relatively close to us, only scorching the floorboards.

"I'm only keeping it contained," Dex answered my unspoken question.

"How?" I gaped at him. "How did you know?"

Giving me a sad smile, Dex brushed the back of his hand against my cheek where tears came off with it. "Because I'd reacted the same way when I found out that's what they'd done to me."

"To you?"

He huffed a laugh. "Except I failed. I wasn't what they wanted, and so they tried again. With you."

Still a bit dumbfounded, I stared at him while my mind whirled. They'd made me. On purpose. And not even the one time. They'd done it to Dex too. What kind of fucked up person would do this?

But they weren't people. They were angels.

CHAPTER 20

I SPENT THE rest of Saturday and Sunday going through the books Dex left me. Ayden had come by a few times to check on me, but I reassured her that I was fine. Just got some upsetting news.

Thankfully, it was enough to keep her from checking up on me the rest of the weekend. There was so much on my mind that I just couldn't handle all the questions and energy that came with socializing.

Dex, the saint, came by with food periodically throughout the day. He seemed to understand that I needed time alone. Of course he would, though. He'd been me not too long ago. Dex knew exactly how I was feeling right now.

The books didn't have a whole lot of information that was useful to me. It was basically filled with a lot of doom and gloom. The prophecy didn't say who the Watcher was, only that they would see the end of times and be able to change it based on their will. I hadn't changed a vision in my life.

Until…the other day.

Never in my life had I ever changed a vision I had from coming true. Not even when my neighbor's dog was about to be run over by a car. It had been so small. It should have been simple to keep it from happening, and yet, my yelling for the cute little Pomeranian to watch out had only caused the dog to rush into the street as it happily ran toward me.

And yet, I had been able to stop Dharma from dumping the milk shake on Cass. In truth, that could have gone better. I still hadn't been able to salvage my favorite jeans because of it.

I still had so many questions and not enough answers. I knew I would have to talk to my dad or Azazel to get them, but I wasn't going to hang around her office waiting for him to show. I'd done enough waiting on my dad in my life.

Chewing on my lower lip, I considered what I could do while I waited. I couldn't stay in my room forever. I'd already missed morning classes. Everyone was probably talking shit about me now, like how I couldn't bear to show my face after I ruined the weekend for everyone.

Like it was even my fault. Dharma, of course, got none of the blame.

I sighed and stood. Figuring I could get a smoke in before I faced everyone at lunch, I grabbed my pack of cigarettes and shoved it in my back pocket. My hand automatically went for my cellphone, but I then remembered I still didn't have it. Something else I'd have to talk to my dad about.

Soon.

I walked out of my room with my head held high. I wasn't about to let anyone make me feel bad about myself. None of this weekend had been my fault. Dharma was the one to blame. If she hadn't had such a chip on her shoulder about the whole putting her in a coma thing, then none of this would have happened. Which was also her fault for putting her nose where it didn't belong.

There were a few stragglers in the hallway on my way outside, but most of them gave me one look and hurried the other way. I suppose fear was better than ridicule. If I had to choose between the two of them… After all, I was used to people being afraid of me.

Determined not to let it bother me, I forced myself not to walk faster and to keep an even unhurried pace. It wasn't until I reached the courtyard full of statues that I finally relaxed.

My boots thudded against the stone walkway as I made my way to the weeping angel. If anyone knew my pain, it would be that guy.

Wasting no time in lighting up, I breathed a big exhale of sweet sweet relief.

Azazel hadn't told me when my dad would be showing up. The anxiety of not knowing and waiting for him to appear so I could give him a piece of my mind was agonizing. I'd stayed up most of the previous nights, practicing what I would say to him.

Did you ever even love Mom? Did you love me? Why? Why? Why?

That was the million-dollar question.

Why?

For power? To finally take down the angels and rule...Heaven? Earth? I didn't know enough about celestial politics to know what the end game actually was. I only knew what those books Dex gave me told me.

The Watcher would see the end of the world and change it to their will. With me being the Watcher.

I snorted to myself.

It was kind of ironic when I thought about it.

The Watcher. Really? Me?

I'd done nothing but watch the people I knew, the people I loved, and those I didn't die over and over again until I didn't want to leave my house. The fact that my entire existence depended on me watching the rest of the world burn was just plain hilarious.

But I wasn't just a watcher now, was I?

My mind drifted to the library and what had happened with Dex. I'd created flames.

Me! I'd never thought I'd be able to do anything like that in my life, and yet...

I pulled my cigarette from my mouth and stared at the tip, willing it to burn like I'd seen Dex do before.

After a long minute of staring, I huffed in annoyance, muttering to myself about being ridiculous.

"It takes practice."

My head jerked up, and I half expected to see Dex there as he usually was, but the voice came from outside the metal fence.

"Cass?" My brows rose with the pitch of my voice.

"In the flesh." Cass chuckled, wrapping his hands around the bars of the fence. His golden blond hair was pulled back today in a small ponytail at the nape of his neck. He wore a worn out dark brown leather jacket with matching boots, and his jeans hugged that fabulous ass. What surprised me was the motorcycle sitting a few paces away from the fence.

"How did you even get here?" I finally asked once I stopped gaping, then I realized what he'd said. "Wait, you know about—"

"Angels, magic, and all that?" Cass arched a brow and smirked. "Well, yeah."

"You said you didn't believe in that crap." I narrowed my eyes at him in accusation.

Cass cocked his head to the side. "I lied."

I stared at him for a long minute and then asked slowly, "Who are you?"

He opened his mouth to answer, but I stopped him.

"And no lies. Fuck knows, I've been lied to enough these days." I took a long drag from my cigarette before dropping it to the ground to stomp it out.

Cass chuckled once more. "Alright, then. My name is Cassiel, but my friends call me Cass. And I'm an—"

"Angel," I finished for him, crossing my arms over my chest. "Yeah, I got it."

He arched a brow.

"Every angel has the stupid -el at the end of their name. God putting his little stamp on all of his creations. At least, the ones he cares about."

Cass seemed surprised by my knowledge. "What about Lucifer? His name doesn't end in -el."

I walked slowly over to the gate and stopped just out of touching distance. "Trick question. His name wasn't originally Lucifer. It was changed after he fell from heaven. Before, it was Samael."

"Ah, so they do teach you lot something in there." Cass smiled, pleased at my answer.

Clicking my tongue, I shifted just a bit closer. "Yep. They also watch your every movement and put little shock collars on you, so you don't go wandering off." I showed him the bracelet on my wrist that I hadn't had a chance to get Azazel to take off yet.

Cass huffed a laugh.

"What?"

Shaking his head, Cass held onto the bars and leaned away so he was almost swinging on them. "Nothing, just for a bunch of rebels they sure do have control issues."

I snorted. "Tell me about it."

"Then why don't you leave?" Cass stopped swinging and locked eyes with me. "Just walk out the front door?"

I waved the bracelet in response. "I have this for one, which I hope to get off today, but secondly..." I reached out and touched the fence, my hand bouncing off of it before I could even reach it. "Can't get through the barrier without a faculty member to lower it."

"Ah." Cass leaned close and placed his forehead against the metal bars. "If you could get the barrier down and that bracelet off, would you?"

"Would I what?"

"Leave."

I gave him a suspicious look before getting as close to the fence as I could. "In a heartbeat."

Though, as I said the words, guilt tugged at my heart. There were reasons to stay. Several in fact, but my dad's betrayal was hard to ignore. He didn't even give me a choice in the matter. He just picked what side I'd be on and kept me in the dark so I couldn't make up my own mind.

Shifting the conversation, I backed up a few steps. "Don't your kind want to kill me?"

Cass gave me a panty melting smile, tucking his hands into the pockets of his jeans. "Why ever would I want to do that?"

"Because I'm an abomination," I supplied for him. "At least, that's what Michael called me."

He laughed. "Michael has a big ole stick up his ass. Not all of us think like that. Besides…" His lips curled up ever so slightly. "You're the Watcher."

"So, you knew who I was when we met?"

Shrugging a shoulder, Cass gave me a knowing look. "Perhaps I had my suspicions and all I had to do to confirm them was to follow your little group of misfits back here."

I shrugged. "That's just what I was told."

"Well…you can't believe everything you hear." He cocked a brow and smirked, then paused and angled his head to the side. "Well, I better be going. I'll see you around, Watcher."

I unabashedly watched the way his pants hugged his ass as Cass walked back to his motorcycle. He threw his leg over it and winked at me before the engine roared to life and he drove away.

Not even a minute later, Ayden came outside. "Hey, there you are. I've been looking all over for you."

I glanced away from where Cass had disappeared from. "I'm right here. What's up?"

She gave me a curious look but then said, "Your dad's here."

Well, that was convenient. I darted a look back to the fence, wondering if Cass knew that my dad had arrived.

"You okay?" Ayden stepped up beside me. "I know you've had a rough weekend, but things will look up soon. Trust me. Plus, your dad's here." She smiled brightly at me. "That's got to count for something, right?"

I didn't remind Ayden that my dad and I had a strained relationship at best, but now that I knew he'd been using me this whole time, I wasn't exactly sure what we had anymore. Instead, I forced a smile to my face and nodded. "Right. Let's go. I want to get this thing off me and get my phone back."

"Ugh." Ayden made a face at my bracelet. "I got that thing taken off the moment I got back. I don't know how you kept it on all weekend."

I lifted a shoulder and dropped it, frowning. "I had a lot on my mind."

She nodded. "I get ya. Dharma was such a bitch at the diner. Then on the bus, she spent the whole time talking shit about you to anyone and everyone who would listen.

You're so lucky you got to ride back with Dex." Ayden sighed happily, as if she would have enjoyed it a bit more than I did.

"Yeah, lucky," I muttered as we walked into the school. "And don't worry about Dharma. She's just an attention whore." I told her with a shake of my head. "There are more important things to worry about."

"Yeah, you're right. Like that hottie, Cass, from town." Ayden clasped her hands in front of her, letting out a dreamy giggle. "I could think of a thing or two I'd like him to study, if you know what I mean."

I winced. I did.

Not wanting to burst Ayden's bubble, I kept silent on the whole Cass was actually an angel bit. At least, it did explain why I was so drawn to him. The whole celestial attraction apparently worked both ways on Nephilim. Too bad it didn't make my dad any more likable. I didn't know how I was going to get through this conversation without burning the whole place to ash.

CHAPTER 21

A PART OF me felt like I was walking to a guillotine. Each step that I took along the hallway was like a punch to my gut. Everyone stared and whispered as I walked by, no doubt talking about this weekend.

I tried to hold back an eye roll, but it was oh so hard.

Ayden followed along beside me, chatting normally about what happened while I was gone, what I'd missed in class, and so on. Her voice became background noise, and I stopped pretending to listen to her as Azazel's office came into view.

"Hey," I interrupted Ayden, placing a hand on her arm. "I just want you to know that whatever happens, I'm glad you became my friend."

Then I did something I never did.

I hugged her.

Laughing slightly, Ayden hugged me back. "I don't know what brought this on, but I'm glad you're my friend too."

Releasing her, I walked over to the office door and knocked. Azazel's voice answered, telling me to come in. I twisted slightly back to Ayden and gave her a small wave and smile.

Confusion covered her face, but she returned both.

Entering Azazel's office, I saw my dad sitting on the couch I had woken up on the first day here. I pushed back the need to run over to him and berate him with questions. I wasn't a child. I wouldn't get answers from these people by acting like one.

Walking up to Azazel's desk where she waited, I held my arm out. "Can you remove this please?"

Azazel exchanged a look with my dad, and for a moment, I thought they weren't going to do it. Then with a flick of her finger, the bracelet fell off.

I kept the sigh of relief from coming out, but couldn't resist rubbing my wrist where it had been.

"Elle," my dad began, standing from the couch to approach me. "I understand you wanted to speak to me."

I scanned him over in his pristine suit and jacket, noticing there wasn't a mark on him. "You don't even look like you've been in battle."

"I told you he was fine," Azazel interjected with a disapproving frown. "Is that all you wanted him for? He has more important things to do than—"

"Azazel." My dad's voice stopped her, his gaze sharp on the other angel. To me, his face softened. "Elle, what's wrong? I heard you've been fighting? And you caused another student to go into a coma?"

My jaw clenched tight, and I wanted to glare at Azazel for tattling, but knew it wouldn't help me right now. "I'm not exactly the same as everyone else here, as you know."

He nodded in understanding. "Yes, I know, but you must try to get along with the others. You may need them in the future."

My fingers curled into fists, but I kept them down at my sides. I tried to keep my voice as neutral as possible as I bit out, "Fine. Can I have my phone back?"

This time, my dad exchanged a look with Azazel and then gave me one of those looks parents do. The one that said, 'I'm doing this for your own good, even if you hate me for it.' How he even knew that look was beyond me. He'd never acted like a parent one day in his life.

"Elle...Eleanor..." My dad sighed and placed his hands on my shoulders.

A flash of something hit me, but not like my other visions. It was only a small hit. A flash of lightning and a wing. Nothing else. It'd be disappointing, except I'd never had a vision when touching my dad. Never. Not once.

"Are you alright?" my dad asked, rubbing my shoulders in what I guessed he thought was a soothing manner. "Are you getting sick?"

"I'm fine." I swallowed thickly. He'd never even bothered to keep from touching me. Did he think that I couldn't get visions of his death? Or did he just not care? Either way, I wasn't about to share with him what I'd just seen. "My phone?"

"You won't be needing it." He dropped his hands from my shoulders and adjusted his suit jacket. "I've taken care of your friend problem. You don't have to worry about her freaking out as you say." He gave me a small smile, obviously pleased with himself.

My heart fell to my stomach, and my hands shook as I barely got out, "What do you mean, she's been dealt with? What did you do?"

"Now, Eleanor..." My dad held a hand up and tried to explain, or rather, lie to me.

"What. Did. You. Do?" I practically shouted in his face, no longer playing the dutiful daughter.

Sighing with annoyance, he dropped his good father act, and my dad locked eyes with me. "I removed you from her memory. She won't come looking for you, and neither will the rest of your mother's family. So, you can stop worrying about them and focus on your studies. Here. Where you are safe."

I stared at him for a long moment, not believing what I had just heard. Then a maniacal laugh spilled forth from my lips, and I clutched my stomach, unable to stop it.

"Eleanor?" My dad frowned and reached for me. "Elle?"

I slapped his hand away from me and swiped at my eyes, which had begun to tear up. "You don't care about me at all, do you?" I swung around to glare at Azazel and him. "All you care about is keeping me on your side of this stupid war."

"What are you blathering on about?" My dad huffed and crossed his arms in annoyance. "You're my daughter. Of course, I care about you."

"Then why? Why?" I screamed at my dad, anger swelling inside of me. "Why did she have to die? Why is any of this happening to me? I'm just an ordinary girl. I never asked for this power." I backed away from him and toward them door. "If you and the angels want my powers so badly, then you can just have it and leave me out of it."

"It doesn't work that way, Elle. We can't control the future, as you know," my dad said, as he tried to soothe my rage.

"Don't touch me." I swung my fist at him. "You're just like the rest of them. Angels. Fallen angels." I shook my head. "Nephilim. You're all alike." I felt power build up inside of me as my insides burned. "Mark my words. You'll regret the day you ever created me."

I ran from the room before he could stop me, my eyes burning with unshed tears.

He didn't care. Not at all. I'd hoped that talking to him would help. That I could somehow understand what he was doing. Why he had lied to me.

In a perfect world, he would have hugged me close, told me it was all for my own good, and that he loved me and my mom more than anything in this world.

Except he hadn't.

There was no use pretending that he would be anything other than what he had always been.

The hallway blurred by as I ran, my feet pounding on the stone floors beneath my feet. Tears streamed down my face as my heart pumped harder. I had to get out of the school. I had to get away from this place. I could feel that burning inside that had come before with Dex.

If my one experience with this feeling told me anything, it was that something was going to get blown up in the next few moments. Except this time, I didn't have Dex to help me control it.

So, I did the only thing I knew to do. I headed for the courtyard. It was large enough that I wouldn't hurt anyone other than the statues and foliage, and let's be honest, no one was going to miss them.

A voice called my name on the way out the door, but I didn't stop. I had to get out. I had to be able to finally...

I reached the middle of the courtyard.

...let go.

A scream ripped from my throat as I threw my arms out to both sides. Every inch of me burned as the world around me turned to molten flames. The grass and bushes turned to ash. The statues melted on their posts.

Even the stone beneath my feet scorched from the power that unleashed from inside of me.

"Elle!"

Dex's voice broke through my rage, and I turned to face him, the flames around me licking the edges of him. He didn't flinch away.

"What happened?" Dex took a step closer and then winced. It seemed my fire could hurt him.

I shook my head, unable and not wanting to talk about it. "I can't. I just can't." I shifted around so I didn't have to face him.

He let out a pained sound, making me jerk back around. He was trying to get past my fire.

"Stop it. You're hurting yourself," I growled at him, and then as suddenly as the fire had appeared around me, it dispersed. Frowning at how easily I had extinguished it, I rushed to Dex's side.

He clutched his arm close to himself. "It's fine. Don't worry about it."

I grabbed his arm and saw the melted flesh. "No, you're not. Why would you do that?"

Dex's lip ticked up on one side. "I can't stand by and let one of my students destroy the whole school, now can I?"

I stared up at him in disbelief as his other hand stroked my hair, much closer than he'd ever let himself get. "But I thought you weren't going to let the vision come true." I mimicked his words back to him, using my best Dex voice.

His brows furrowed together as he frowned thoughtfully. "I've fought fate my entire life, I'm tired of fighting." He cupped my chin and stared deep into my eyes. "And you, Elle Richmond... I think fate has a helluva lot more instore for both of us."

I swallowed hard, not sure how to respond to his proclamation. No one had ever said anything like that to me before. Sure, guys had been happy to jump in the sack with the weirdo girl, but none of them had ever walked through fire for me.

Too stumped by what he'd said, I allowed him to press his lips to mine. Before either of us could deepen the kiss, he pulled back.

"We can't. Not here." He took my hand and led me toward the school. "Let's go to—"

An explosion shook the ground and the remnants of the courtyard. Dex clasped me tight while we tried to keep on our feet.

"What was that?" I asked after the rumbling stopped.

Before Dex could answer, an alarm sounded over the academy. Worry crossed over Dex's face, and he pushed me toward the door.

"You need to get inside. Go, hide. And don't come out until I come find you."

Except I wasn't about to have anything decided for me anymore. Not now, not ever.

"Not until you tell me what's going on."

Dex looked like he was going to argue, but then saw my face and sighed. "The angels. They're here."

CHAPTER 22

SCREAMS FROM BACK inside the school pulled my attention, and I hurried through the doors. The academy shook again, causing dust and bits of ceiling to fall down around me.

Dex hadn't followed me inside. I assumed they had some kind of plan in place for if angels attacked, and he was doing his duties.

I had to worry about me.

Rushing through the hallways, I found Ayden and the others coming out of the dining room.

"Elle!" Ayden raced over to me. "What's going on?"

"Angels," I told her, my lips pressed tight together, and then I looked to the others. "Is there somewhere we're supposed to go if this happens?"

Joash stepped up with an arm wrapped around Coral. "Yeah, we're all to go to the library. There's a secret entrance into some underground tunnels there."

"Well then, let's go!" I swung an arm for them to follow me. Why I thought I was the leader now, I didn't know, but something in me said I had to get them to safety before anything else.

The hallways were crowded as we worked our way from the dining hall to the library. Everyone else apparently knew the drill. It made me wonder if they had normal fire drills like this—but for angels.

Everyone was so close that it was impossible not to brush up against anyone. My jaw clenched and my nails bit into my hands as I was assaulted with vision after vision. One of them hit me so hard that it knocked me off my feet and into someone nearby.

"What the hell, freak? Get off!"

Hands shoved at me as I blinked my vision clear. It was Dharma. Of course I would run into her now. Not having time for her high school drama, I held my hands up and steadied myself. "Sorry."

"You better be." She sniffed and then scowled. "What are you doing here anyway? This passage is for students. Not freaks like you."

"Knock it off, Dharma." Zephyr stepped between us with a glare. "This isn't the time for games. The angels are coming and—"

"And who do you think they are coming for?" Dharma interrupted him, stepping into his personal space. "Her." She pointed a finger at me. "They're attacking us and our home because of her. Everything bad that has happened lately has all been because of her," she snarled and tried to push past Zephyr to get in my face, but he kept her away. "Why don't you just go to them and leave us in peace? Things were better before you got here."

"Dharma," Zephyr growled, and this time, his brother stepped up with him. "Just go."

With a harrumph, Dharma spun on her heel and marched into the library.

I stood silent as I watched her go. I wished I could say she was wrong. That all the badness wasn't my fault, but I knew it was. It always was. It was part of my life. I'd never known anything other than pain, death, and despair. Why should now be any different?

"Don't let her bother you." Zephyr moved over to me, giving me a small encouraging smile. "She's just pissed that Dex is finally noticing a student and it's not her."

I opened my mouth to argue we weren't doing anything, but then closed it and shook my head. "Don't worry about it. She doesn't bother me. Come on." I jerked my head toward the library. "Let's get everyone to safety."

"You too, right?" Ayden touched my arm, concern on her face. When I didn't answer immediately, she dropped her hand, her face falling with understanding. "I see. That's what that hug was all about before."

"No, I—" I began, but then stopped. "I have to find out what's going on. If it's really about me, it wouldn't be right for me to run away."

"I understand." Ayden's eyes teared up, and she threw herself around me. "Be careful, okay?"

I patted her on the head. "I'll do my best."

Pulling away, she wiped her nose with her sleeve. "You better do more than that."

I smiled sadly.

Bayu pulled her away from me and into his arms. "We'll take care of her, don't worry." I pushed my lips into some semblance of grateful before watching him walk her away.

Coral reached for me but kept herself from touching me. "It was nice meeting you, Elle."

"This isn't goodbye," I told her, causing her to bawl into Joash's chest. He gave me one of those little guy acknowledgments when they were too cool to have feelings.

I laughed and waved.

That only left Zephyr.

"Walk me to the tunnel?" he asked, though I knew it was a façade, but I agreed anyway.

While the building still shook around us and the alarm blared its lungs off, the students had mostly gotten out and into the tunnels already, leaving the library deserted.

We stopped by a bookshelf that had been opened some secret way, leading up into a dark stairway.

Staring into the dark abyss of the hidden passageway, I had a sinking feeling. "Where do the tunnels go?"

Zephyr shrugged. "I don't know for sure. We've never had to use them. Somewhere near town probably." We went quiet for a moment, and then he asked, "Are you going to be okay?"

I smirked, but it was forced. "Aren't I always?"

He huffed a laugh. "That's the thing with you. Always hiding how much you need others behind your badassery. One of these days, you're going to find yourself very much alone and no one to help you."

My expression fell. "Yeah. Well, that day isn't today."

"No," Zephyr agreed, patting me on the back. "It's not today. Watch your back out there, alright?"

I bobbed my head and stepped back from the tunnels. "You too. I'll see you again."

Zephyr winked. "Count on it."

Waiting until he disappeared into the darkness, I let myself have a moment before twisting on my heel and heading back out of the library.

The academy was holding up pretty well, all things considered. They must have put up a pretty strong barrier if all that banging around hadn't destroyed the building around us.

Still, I had to watch my step as I jogged through the hallways and back toward the front of the academy. The initial blast had sounded like it had come from there, so that's where all the action would be.

There were teachers hiding near the front door, but none of them paid me any mind as I went past. One door was off its hinges and lying on the ground. The other one stood ajar.

I was temporarily blinded as I stepped outside. Standing still as I waited for my eyes to adjust, I used my other senses to figure out what was going on.

Familiar voices shouted and commands were given.

"Fire workers, over there," Azazel ordered from the left.

On my other side, my dad's voice called out, "Wind workers, bring them down to your level."

A fire ball hurled through the air and through the barrier as if it didn't exist. The angels, all dressed in some form of armor, dodged and parried them like they weren't even breaking a sweat. Which was unfortunate for the Nephilim on the ground, who looked like they were about to collapse from their efforts.

Dex was among them.

My feet immediately started for him, but a sound in the distance caught my attention.

The rumbling roar of an engine filled my ears moments before Cass pulled up to the front gate. The visual of him there was quite something to behold.

He sat there on his motorcycle with the gleam of his wings barely visible to the naked eye. He was like a warrior on a chariot of fire, waiting to whisk me away from it all.

As if reading my mind, the barrier around us fell.

He didn't call out to me, he just waited there for me to make my decision.

This was my chance. This was what I wanted all along. I had the chance to get away from this school, away from my dad, and a chance to decide for myself.

My gaze darted to Dex and my dad for a brief second. Only Dex realized what was going on, his eyes locking with mine through the rubble of the front courtyard around us. He forced himself up and ran toward me.

Before my mind could tell my body it had made a decision, I darted across the courtyard.

I jumped over destroyed statues and dodged angel blasts. They apparently didn't care who they hit, as long as they did some damage. I tucked that away for later as I raced toward my freedom.

Cass waited on the back of his motorcycle. It roared as he revved the engine. "Come on, 'lil Watcher." He smirked at me as I climbed onto the back of his bike.

"Elle, no!" Dex shouted as he chased after me, but he was too late.

"Go, go!" I wrapped my arms around Cass's waist and then was almost knocked out of my seat by the vision that hit me square in the chest.

Cass held me close, his wings wrapped around our naked bodies as we moved together as one. It sent a burning rush of heat to my core and a blush to my face.

"You're not a mind reader, are you?" I shouted over the wind as he roared away from the school, the sound of the battle fading into the distance.

"No, why?" he called over his shoulder.

I held him tighter and muttered, "No reason. Just get me out of here."

Find what kind of trouble Elle gets herself into in Fire In Her Blood!

About the Author

Erin Bedford is an otaku, recovering coffee addict, and Legend of Zelda fanatic. Her brain is so full of stories that need to be told that she must get them out or explode into a million screaming chibis. Obsessed with fairy tales and bad boys, she hasn't found a story she can't twist to match her deviant mind full of innuendos, snarky humor, and dream guys.

On the outside, she's a work from home mom and bookbinger. One the inside, she's a thirteen-year-old boy screaming to get out and tell you the pervy joke they found online. As an ex-computer programmer, she dreams of one day combining her love for writing and college credits to make the ultimate video game!

Until then, when she's not writing, Erin is devouring as many books as possible on her quest to have the biggest book gut of all time. She's written over thirty books,

ranging from paranormal romance, urban fantasy, and even scifi romance.
Also, third person is really weird when writing about yourself. Just putting that out there.

Come chat me up!
www.erinbedford.com
Facebook.com/erinrbedford
twitter.com/erin_bedford
Don't forget to follow me on Goodreads, Pinterest, Instagram, and YouTube!

Want to be the first to know about my new releases?
Erinbedford.com/newsletter